Praise for Edgar Award–winning
Mark Sadler

"Mark Sadler writes of despair and violence with sizable narrative talents."

—*New York Times*

"Mark Sadler knows both the topside and underside of the New York scene. He writes about both with intelligently controlled ferocity and speed."

—Ross Macdonald

"His style has a distinctive resonance all its own."
—*San Francisco Chronicle*

"Sadler knows his onions when it comes to Private Investigators. His Paul Shaw is flesh and blood."

—*Book World*

"... fresh and young and powerful a voice. [His novels are] distinguished by their own unique voice in the service of the writer's own unique viewpoint."

—Warren B. Murphy

Circle of Fire

MARK SADLER

BERKLEY BOOKS, NEW YORK

To the Remaks,
Roberta and Herr Doktor Professor

1

FROM THE DARKENED theater, among the glittering first-night audience, I watched her on the stage—Maureen Shaw, my wife. But someone else now. Not my wife, not even the actress, but the sad, tortured, towering character in the play. At work, creating her truth and beauty. Pain up there onstage, and yet I felt good. Alive.

Perhaps because once you have ached to be an artist, as I had, great art like Maureen's always gives hope. A dark beauty, and yet true, and when the curtain dropped I felt good. I felt intoxicated, higher than any drug-high, as I went backstage to stand in Maureen's dressing room and watch all those who came to honor her work. Maureen Shaw, actress. My wife. Later . . .

John Thayer came into the dressing room.

"Delaney's been shot," he said. "Three hours ago. Los Angeles just called."

2

MAUREEN IS MY wife, it was her opening night. But Dick Delaney is my partner—*Thayer, Shaw and Delaney- Security and Investigations*, New York and Los Angeles— and it was just past 2 A.M. when John Thayer and I walked into the Los Angeles hospital room. The miracle of jet flight.

Our L.A. secretary, Mildred, stood over the bed where Dick Delaney lay under an oxygen tent. His boy and girl— nine and seven—sat in a corner. Their mother is dead. John Thayer went to them.

"He's still in a coma, Paul," Mildred said. "Critical, but the doctors say there's hope."

"Yes," I said.

Thayer said, "Someone has to take over his work."

He's a hunter, John Thayer, a cool machine behind his rimless glasses.

I took Mildred out into the corridor, lit a cigarette. Mildred wasn't crying, she knew our work, what we had to do.

"It happened in our parking lot, Paul. I heard the

shots. No one saw anyone. He hasn't been able to say anything.''

"What was he working on?"

"Only two cases. A Saul Mashler hired us to investigate his son, and the bomb murder of a state senator up in Fort Smith. Dick just started on both of them.''

"Did he talk about them? Anything?"

"No, but this was in his pocket.''

It was a page from Delaney's memo pad. An address and nothing more: 148 Ashford Way.

"That's in Pacific Palisades,'' Mildred said.

"All right, let's look at the files.''

Los Angeles is never asleep. The fast cars, bright women and hungry men out at any hour. But there was little traffic on Wilshire, and our office building was deserted behind its glass lobby doors. Mildred made coffee in the office while I read the two files. A thousand old enemies could have shot Delaney, but it was a ninety-nine percent chance that the answer was in one of the current cases. We had to go on anyway, our job.

There wasn't much in the files. Young Craig Mashler had been staying away from his Brentwood home, sneaking in late. Delaney had hired a legman, Leo Cohn, to tail the boy. The only report showed that Craig Mashler hung out in teenage joints, went to the beach a lot—even now in October. Not unusual in Southern California.

The state senator—Russell Dobson, Republican—had been bombed with a woman in a tavern parking lot at exactly 6:02 P.M. one week ago. His campaign manager, Campbell Grant, had hired us two days ago because he wanted a detective from far away. If politics was involved, that was logical.

There was nothing in either file about the Pacific Palisades address.

When Mildred brought the coffee, I told her to call the legman, Leo Cohn. She got no answer. I sent her home, finished the coffee, decided to try the Mashler boy first, slept on the couch.

3

A CLEAR MORNING in Brentwood, warm for October, and I saw the cars in front of the Mashler house. Four long black limousines. Knots of people dressed in black. When I asked for Saul Mashler, they stared at me as if I were guilty of something.

Saul Mashler stood in the center of a big living room where all the furniture matched as if it had been bought in a block with the walls included like an expensive set of books no one read. A small man with fat hands and a stunned face, he watched a group of women who hovered over a thin bleached blonde with a face ten years too old for her hair. As I walked to him, Mashler looked at his watch but made no move to go anywhere.

"Craig?" I said. "How?"

He blinked at me.

"Thayer, Shaw and Delaney," I said. "You hired us to investigate him. I'm Paul Shaw."

"Yes," he said. A kind of wonder in his voice as if he had hired us so long ago.

"What happened, Mr. Mashler?"

"Dead," he said. "I mean . . . Craig." He looked at his watch, at the thin blond woman, at me. "What do you want? You got paid, didn't you? The other guy, I paid him for a week. There isn't any job now."

"The 'other guy' was shot last night," I said. "He was working for you. How did your son die, Mr. Mashler?"

"Mr. Delaney?" Mashler said. "Is he—?"

"He's alive," I said. "Barely. I want to know—"

"No," Saul Mashler said. "Drugs. Dirty, stupid drugs! Just him, Craig, stealing for drug money. He took too much. Too much!"

"On his own? No gang? You're sure?"

"Alone. Cops said so. All . . . alone."

"When did it happen?" I tried to make my voice gentle. His son was dead from some need he didn't understand. With all the words, it still can't happen to us, no.

"Three days ago. We needed time before . . . My wife, she needed time. Now we bury him."

"I'm sorry, Mr. Mashler," I said.

It was as good as anything. Whatever I said would be without meaning. As I walked out to our company car, I was sorry—and glad, too. Craig Mashler had been a lone kid on drugs, dead two days before Delaney had been shot. There couldn't be any connection. It narrowed down my work a lot. A tragedy for Saul Mashler, a break for me.

4

THE SUN WAS hot in Pacific Palisades. Number 148 Ashford Way was a large garden-apartment complex on the rim of a canyon of heavy brush with a highway being built down at the bottom. At least fifty apartments in two-story blocks around a green court and a swimming pool. The manager was in the office. A friendly little man at a cluttered desk. He nodded over my credentials.

"Sure, I remember your partner. Left his card, said I should call him if I remembered anything."

"About what?"

"Man named Russell Dobson, or a town called Fort Smith."

"Have you remembered anything?"

"Nope. I don't recall anyone named Dobson around here, senator or not. No tenant like that. Your partner even described this Dobson, and that rang no bells."

"You ever have a tenant from Fort Smith?"

"He asked that, too. None I know, and I've been here for five years. I hardly even heard of Fort Smith."

"Did my partner say why he was looking for Dobson here?"

"Nope."

"You told him nothing more than you've told me?"

" 'Nothing' is the right word."

"Was anyone else asking for Dobson at any time? Did anyone ask for my partner after he was here? Anything at all odd?"

"No, I can't say there was." He thought. "Except, well, there was a car, maybe. After your partner left here, I saw a parked car maybe go off after him. Not many cars park out on the street there. It's no parking, and we've got a lot."

"What kind of car? Who was in it?"

"Can't say. An impression was all I got. Can't be sure I saw anything. Could just as easily have been nothing."

He was right. Still—someone had shot Dick Delaney.

I thanked him, went back to my car and took the long way to our Wilshire office along Sunset and La Cienega. Mildred was waiting for me in Delaney's office.

"The Dobson bomb murder," I said, sat behind Delaney's desk. "Has to be. How is he?"

"No change. They say that's good."

"The kids?"

"At their house with Thayer. I'm getting a woman to stay with them so Thayer can go back to New York," Mildred said. "You think it was the Dobson case?"

"Unless it was an old grudge." I sensed news in her face. "Why? What's happened?"

She held out a letter. "This came this morning."

A business-size envelope, and a Fort Smith postmark. The letterhead and signature belonged to Campbell Grant, Attorney—the campaign manager who had hired Delaney. Grant got to the point without frills—he was calling us off the case. He had been confused by the loss of his friend, distraught. There was no need for us, the sheriff up there was handling it fully, Grant had every confidence in the sheriff. There was a check for two hundred dollars to cover what his retainer hadn't.

"It's addressed to Dick," I said, "but could Grant know that Dick's been shot?"

"Not unless he knows who shot him, or did it himself," Mildred said. "Thayer told me to keep it quiet."

Thayer always kept his head, cool and precise.

"I wonder which side the sheriff up there is on?" I said. "I guess I better go up and find out."

"We don't have a client now, Paul."

"Yes, we have—Delaney."

"If he was shot over the Dobson case."

"I won't find out down here. Call my wife and tell her I'll call her at the theater about eleven her time."

5

AT 8 P.M. IT was dark, and I was north of San Francisco. I stopped at a motel outside the town of Bodega Bay, checked in and called Maureen. She wasn't happy. She had received rave reviews, the play hadn't, and where the hell was I?

"I'm sorry, darling," she said. "Will Dick live?"

"I hope so."

"Call me when you can."

I had dinner at a good restaurant that overlooked the sea. A rocky shore up here, white spray high as the waves rolled in down below the cliffs. Wonderful scenery, and good striped bass, but I was thinking of Dick Delaney. Only two days on the Dobson case. What could he have learned? Maybe nothing—someone who wanted to be sure he never did learn anything. Or I could be fishing in empty waters.

Detectives make enemies who hold grudges. Most of them do nothing about it, but once in a while one does. Then it's a job of checking all the back cases, finding out where all the old enemies are now, and which one had had a big enough grudge and the opportunity. A long, dirty job if Fort Smith proved barren.

After dinner I walked along the cliffs. The white sea flashed below in the thin moonlight. A harsh, restless coast; a ponderous sea battling the drenched rocks that stood up like barbarian outriders defending the dark land behind them. I walked for an hour in the sound of the sea on the rocks, stopped for a drink at a tavern on the highway, and went to bed. I wanted an early start for Fort Smith.

I came awake to the faint sound of a car door closing. Steps somewhere out in the brush that surrounded the rural motel. One man who stopped outside my door. A sense of presence in the night, as if he were out there staring at my door, considering.

The feel of the night wasn't late. My watch read 11:44. There was traffic on the highway, and voices somewhere near the motel. The man outside moved softly away to the left.

I got up, slipped on my trousers and jacket, got my pistol—a light Colt Agent—and opened the back window of the room. I searched the clear night, my eyes accustomed from the darkened room. I saw no one. I climbed out the window, stepped into the shadows of a grove of small trees.

He came around the corner of the unit. A compact man in a dull leather windbreaker and black slacks. He passed silently through a patch of moonlight toward the rear windows of my room. A black man, the acne pits shadowed on his glistening face, a big pistol in his right hand. He stopped at my rear windows, looked in, his gun raised.

I cocked my little Agent so he could hear it, saw his neck stiffen, his breath hold. He'd heard a pistol cock before.

"Stand there," I said. I stayed in the shadows of the trees. "Throw the gun behind you. Now."

He threw the heavy pistol behind him.

"Turn."

He turned.

"Who are you? Who sent you?"

He said nothing, his sweating black face impassive. But his eyes moved as if looking for a way to run, and his left hand was in a fist. He was scared. I shot at his feet. He jerked back, tried to smile as if he'd been told that when someone tried to scare you, you had to smile. He failed.

"Your name," I said.

He tried to see me in the shadows of the trees. It's better to see danger, know it's human. He couldn't see me. He stayed silent. I shot him in the leg. He went down, cursing.

"What's your name?"

He held his leg, blood on his hands. "Johnny. Johnny Gavin. Christ, man, I'm bleedin' bad!"

He sat up holding tight to the wound. Panic in his eyes.

"Who sent you?"

I cocked my Agent again.

There were three shots, carefully spaced. From my left. The corner of the motel unit. My prisoner screamed once, was flung over sideways from the force of the two shots that hit him, lay still.

The third shot came into my grove of trees. Not near me, but I went down, anyway. From behind a tree I saw nothing at the corner of the motel, nothing anywhere in the night. I heard distant feet on concrete. I got up, ran in the shadow of the trees to the corner of the motel. A car door closed ahead of me, an engine started, the car drove off. I walked out onto the highway with my revolver ready, but the road was empty.

I went back to my prisoner. He was dead. Both shots in

the head. Good shooting. Very good in the dark, even as close as the killer had been. I searched the dead man. He had nothing on him. Stripped, not even any money. I stood up and looked down at him and wondered if he had known, as the bullets hit, that he had been "dead" from the start.

Kill me, or fail, he had been a dead man the moment he came after me. His death had been a sure, neat, professional job. A more professional killer than himself had been behind him all the way. So that when I died my killer died too, or if my killer missed he died, anyway. No suspect to question, no witness, no trail back to whoever hired him.

There was no need for me to call the police. Someone had called already. I heard the sirens, and the motel was a blaze of light as the curious began to come out.

6

THEY WERE SHERIFF'S men. They took me to the sheriff. He listened to my story. I told it straight, all of it. They lent me a cell to sleep in while they went to work. It was almost dawn when the sheriff sent for me again.

"No Johnny Gavin anywhere in this county, no record on him, no one like him. You're sure you didn't know him, Shaw?"

The sheriff was a big burly man in a white Stetson who could have posed for a sheriff in any ad. He looked tired.

"I'm sure," I said. "I didn't think he was a local. I was probably tailed from L.A., or was picked up along the way, maybe in San Francisco. I'm driving a company car anyone could have identified in L.A. and sent word ahead."

"Yeh, we're trying L.A. and San Francisco for an ident on Gavin. Not that it's going to matter much. If we find out who he was, all we'll learn is that he sold his gun to anyone who could pay. The backup man won't help, either, if we could trace him. He won't know who hired Gavin or why. Or who you are."

"No. His only job was to kill Gavin."

The sheriff thought. "Anything to the black angle, Shaw? Race stuff in the Dobson bombing? In your partner's past?"

"No on my partner. I don't know about Fort Smith yet, but I doubt it. Even hired guns have equal opportunity these days."

"Yeh," the sheriff said. "Okay, you checked out and your gun's clean. That backup man used a rifle. We're not going to get far here, or in L.A. or San Francisco. When you know who wants you dead, you'll know who hired this Gavin. Come back and tell us, right?"

I went to the motel for my things, drove on north as the October day began to warm.

7

THE LAST FIFTEEN miles into Fort Smith I drove through Crescent Rocks Redwood State Park. The giant trees towered in the afternoon sun to the left of the highway, the light shafts soft among their straight trunks like the muted pillars of light inside some temple. A silence, as if even sound were awed by the magnificent trees, the sense of timelessness under their branches.

To the right, a forest of lesser trees extended past houses and foothills inland to the mountains of the Coast Range, the Sierra Nevadas, the lakes, the lava beds. They all came together here in the north of the state, the wild country inland where there were few roads and fewer towns.

Then I reached Fort Smith. I knew what it would be like, I know my countrymen, but it was a shock after the beauty of the land. First there were the lumbermills with their smoke and sawdust. The lumberyards, brickyards, supermarkets, feed stores, farm-equipment stores and showrooms. The new tracts and the older frame houses on dusty side streets, and on the eastern slopes the bigger houses of the lumbermen and business leaders. Then the wide main street.

An ugly two-story town with a main street of yellow brick stores, dirty red brick buildings, and square frame buildings with false fronts. A squat functional brick court-house with the inevitable flagpole and cannon. A town that could have been any small city in Ohio or Georgia or Iowa, the setting made no difference. As if the people had come here from Ohio or Iowa with their eyes fixed only on their ledgers and ambitions. Like a sore on the magnificent land, built by blind men who thought they were still on their Midwestern plains. Or by men who didn't care where they were, the land unimportant except for what they could rip from it. A city of lumbermen, ranchers and farmers—and yet not quite.

On the road into town there had been motels and road-houses and elegant restaurants that obviously catered to tourists, vacationers. The hotels and sport shops of a resort area; signs that directed to the beaches, coves and State Park along the shore. A resort city, too, selling its beauty and nature—but to strangers. For the locals it was just another business.

Campbell Grant, the lawyer-manager who had hired Delaney, had his office in a new professional center on the edge of the main business section—lawyers, accountants, tax experts, insurance agents convenient under one roof: solve your problems all in one stop. Campaign posters were still up on the walls of Grant's office. The late Senator Dobson—*He knows his job!* A gray-haired lady presided in the outer office.

"Can I help you?"

"Mr. Delaney to see Mr. Grant."

"You have an appointment?"

"He'll see me."

She was dubious, but she used the telephone. She gave Delaney's name, listened, hung up. "You can go in."

The inner office was large, sunny and well appointed—yet, somehow, insubstantial. Too shiny, the rich furniture giving me a feeling that if I looked I would find the labels still on the pieces somewhere. Something of a front, and the tall man who stood up behind an ebony-black desk gave me the same sensation. Blue eyes amost too steady; thick blond hair just long and grizzled enough to be modernly independent without actually offending the more conservative. A handsome face with a strong chin, and a well-cut dark-blue pinstripe suit. A faint aura of the opportunist, but only in the appearance, the setting. His manner had no con man in it now. He wasn't smiling.

"You're not Delaney. Who are you? How did you know—?"

I sat down. "You hired Thayer, Shaw and Delaney. I'm Shaw. Paul Shaw, out from our New York office."

"All right, but didn't you get my letter?"

"I got it."

"Then why—"

"Delaney was shot two days ago."

Grant sat down. Despite the playboy façade, I guessed he was a pretty good lawyer. He thought before he spoke, studied a situation in his mind, and didn't flinch from conclusions.

"Is he dead?"

"Not yet," I said.

"You think the senator's murder is connected to it?"

"It's the only current case that could be."

Grant turned a pen in his hand, slowly. He not only thought before he spoke, he thought quickly and clearly. It made me think about his calling the case off. He didn't seem to me like a man who would be confused, hire a detective because he was distraught.

"Why a current case?" he said. "People like Delaney, in your business, must have fifty old cases full of enemies."

"Ninety-nine to one that never happens, old enemies don't come back. People kill in fear and anger, Grant, but few of them will, once the moment of fear or anger is gone."

Grant shook his head. "No, it's not possible."

"You couldn't have been followed to Los Angeles?"

"Of course I could have been followed. But Dobson's murder has to be political, probably professional. Delaney hadn't even arrived here, talked to anyone. Political murderers, and professionals, don't panic, strike before they must, take risks."

"You're sure they didn't have an immediate reason to stop Delaney?"

"No, I'm not sure," Grant snapped. "I'm using my best judgment. This wasn't an individual crime. The work of a group. Which group I don't know, and I won't guess. I was stunned, angry, went off half cocked. Now I realize that it's the kind of job the sheriff can do best. Some organized group killed Dobson for political reasons, and such a group wouldn't indulge in murder simply to stop a private investigation."

"Unless Delaney knew something," I said. "Why did Delaney go to 145 Ashford Way in Pacific Palisades to ask for Dobson?"

Campbell Grant got up, stood at his window looking out at a row of older frame houses on a dusty back street. "When I went down to hire him, he asked me to tell him anything and everything even a little unusual Dobson might have done or said. There was almost nothing I could tell him; Dobson kept his private life very quiet, his public life very ordinary and careful. The only unusual incident I could recall in the year I was with him here was a letter he got about nine months ago marked 'Personal.' It shook him more than anything I'd seen, and the return address was 145 Ashford Way. There was no name, I never saw the letter. Dobson left town for a day, no more. He was his normal self when he returned, and he never mentioned the letter.''

"Did he go to Los Angeles the day he was gone?"

"I don't know if where he went had any connection to that letter at all. The address never came up again. I only told Delaney about it because it was all I could think of. For all I know it could have been a bill.''

"What about the political situation up here?"

The ex-campaign manager didn't answer me. Not for a time. He stood at his window with his back to me, his left hand opening and closing. With the afternoon sun on his thick blond hair and broad shoulders he was an imposing figure, the kind the women's clubs love as a speaker. He finally turned to face me.

"There's no need to discuss the political situation here, Mr. Shaw," he said, choosing his words. "I have discharged your firm, paid you in full. I did not ask you to come here, I don't want you here. The sheriff will handle the case, we have no need of outsiders. Dobson's murderer will be found, and if there is any evidence that the shooting of your partner is involved, the sheriff will tell you."

"No," I said and stood up. "Delaney's been shot, he may die. I was attacked last night. Someone wanted me dead, too. When I'm attacked, it's my case."

"You have no proof that Dobson's murder is involved."

"I'll get the proof."

"Not with any help from me!"

"If that's how you want it," I said. "And I'm not so sure I buy your story of why you want us off the case."

"I don't care what you buy, Shaw," Grant snapped. "That has the sound of a threat. You have no client. I can make the sheriff stop a man who threatens me. You understand?"

"Name the best motel in town."

"The Redwood Motor Inn," Grant said and reddened. "Shaw—!"

"If you or the sheriff want me any time, I'll be there."

I walked out.

8

THE REDWOOD MOTOR Inn had two swimming pools and a restaurant, and a rooftop nightclub that overlooked the redwoods and the Pacific. They also had a room for me—it was October. I tried to call Maureen. She didn't answer. I called Mildred in our L.A. office. Delaney was still alive, still unconscious. I had a drink in my room.

I was going to have to work alone, start at the beginning. I'd done it before. The first stop is always the library.

It was a small library in an old frame house up a side street. Fort Smith wasn't a library town. But it had what I needed—the newspapers from the day Dobson was murdered until today. It took less than an hour. There wasn't much.

Senator Russell Dobson had stopped for a drink at a roadhouse, The Pines, at 5:15 P.M. eight days ago—a Monday. He'd arrived alone, met a woman named Lillian Marsak, had two dry Manhattans, and left The Pines bar just before 6 P.M. with the Marsak woman. Apparently they had gone straight to the woman's car, and at 6:02 it blew up with both of them inside. There were plenty of words about political lawlessness and extremist violence, and dark hints of radical "new" elements. That was all— not a word about suspects or suspicions.

On the library lawn I lit a cigarette in the early evening sun. *Her* car. Why not *his* car? It had been there at The Pines, too. The police didn't seem to think it was worth comment. No hint of its being odd. It was odd to me. Unless the police knew something I didn't, it was very odd. That was one thing.

Another was that a bomb has to be planted in advance, so someone had known that Russell Dobson was going to meet Lillian Marsak at The Pines that evening. Someone must have known that when Dobson left the bar he would go with Lillian Marsak to *her* car, not his.

A third thing was, *Why* had Dobson gone to the woman's car? What had their relationship been? Her car because Dobson didn't want his car seen wherever they had been going that evening from The Pines? Or didn't want the woman seen in his car? No one had mentioned a Mrs. Dobson. Whatever, someone had known Dobson well enough to be sure he would go with Lillian Marsak to her car, and someone had known his schedule for that day well enough to know he was meeting Lillian Marsak that evening.

I drove back to the Redwood Inn considering where to start. Since it was after five o'clock, Dobson's office would be closed even if it was still in business. I sat on the bed and looked in the telephone book. Dobson had had an office on Main Street and a home at 27 San Mateo Lane. Even a bachelor had relatives, at least a housekeeper. Or maybe I should begin at The Pines. I had to eat, and The Pines was probably as good as anywhere in Fort Smith. A shower, a fresh shirt, and dinner at The Pines.

I steamed under the hottest water I could stand, and

heard the knocking. A pounding on my room door, faint in the noise of the shower. I took a quick dose of cold water, shut off the shower. While I dried fast, the knocking went on loud and insistent. I threw on the old blue terry-cloth robe Maureen had sent me in Vietnam, and went out to the door.

There were two of them. A small, terrier-type man in a loud yellow-and-blue checked blazer and blue slacks; and a broad, muscular man maybe an inch shorter than my six feet three and about my age, thirtyish, but a good forty pounds heavier than my hundred and ninety, and all of it muscle under a rumpled brown suit. The little man had quick fox eyes, and wore a jaunty Tyrolean hat with a yellow feather. The big one had small, cloudy eyes, and wore a tiny metal medal ribbon in his lapel. I knew the ribbon—the Silver Star. The big man nodded at me.

"He was in the shower, Jack. I told you I heard the shower. He couldn't hear us knockin' in the shower."

"You were right, Ben," the small man, Jack, said.

"He never heard us in the shower, Jack," the big man said.

"No way, you were right," Jack agreed, and said to me, "Do we come in, Shaw?"

"That depends what you want," I said.

"We got an invitation for you, that's all," the little man said.

I nodded, stepped back. They came in and closed the door. I took off my robe and began to dress. The big man looked me over with approval. His small, cloudy eyes were like very shallow water. I sensed that the big man didn't think of very much, but he admired muscles. At thirty-one, I try to keep in shape. The smaller man wasn't concerned with my build.

"I'm Jack Ready, that's Ben Wheeler," he said. "We work for Mr. Vasto. Mr. Vasto wants to see you, okay?"

I stepped into my trousers. "Who's Mr. Vasto?"

"He owns a couple or two things around here," Ready said.

The big one, Wheeler, said, "Hey he don' know Mr. Vasto."

"He's from someplace else, Ben," Jack Ready said.

"L.A., right, Jack? He's from L.A. I been to L.A."

"That's right, Ben," Ready said. "Mr. Vasto says come have dinner on him, Shaw. Okay?"

I tied my tie at the mirror. "How does Mr. Vasto know me?"

"He heard," Ready said.

Ben Wheeler said, "Mr. Vasto he knows everything happens, right, Jack?"

"Not much he don't know, that's right," Jack Ready said.

I put on my suit jacket, holstered my stubby Colt. They both watched me but said nothing. If they knew my name they knew my work, too, and the gun wouldn't surprise them. I wanted them to think I was alert and prepared. The big one, Ben Wheeler, only looked at Jack Ready, licked his heavy lips. They were a team, I realized, and the leader was obvious.

"Okay," I said, "let's have Mr. Vasto's dinner."

9

WE STOPPED AT a roadhouse just north of Fort Smith. When I saw where we were going, I wasn't really surprised. In a small city, an out-of-town detective attracts attention. The reserved neon sign in front of the white frame roadhouse with its parking lots on both sides read: THE PINES.

Mr. Salvatore Vasto greeted me in his office, waved Ready and Wheeler out. He smiled behind a battered old desk.

"Sit down, Mr. Shaw."

Vasto was about forty, of medium height, medium weight, with black hair and dark-brown eyes, and a pleasant, open face. He wore a ready-made gray suit with a gray sweater under it against the October night chill, like some neighborhood businessman in any Italian neighborhood. He seemed relaxed, smoked a thin black Italian cigar. An easygoing Latin temperament.

I sat down. "You own The Pines, Mr. Vasto?"

"Built it myself. Nice, right? Always wanted to open a restaurant—the Italian dream, right? Got a resort hotel on the shore, too, and a lake lodge, and some stores. The tourists, that's what I live on, right?''

"Meaning what?"

He smiled. "You're new here, sure. Okay, you'll figure it out. The Dobson murder, right? Who hired you on it?''

"Campbell Grant."

"Yeh, that figures. What's he do with no candidate?"

"He fired me, too," I said. "Maybe he's got plans even without a candidate."

Vasto eyed me. "But you're staying?"

"Someone shot my partner, tried to shoot me. I stay."

"So?" Arched eyebrows. "Playing for real, someone?"

"Why did you want to talk to me?"

"I got a stake, right? Hey, talking about steak, you hungry?"

"It can wait," I said. "What stake do you have?"

"What do you know about Dobson? Politics here? The sides?"

"Nothing. Dobson was the incumbent Republican senator."

"Republican? Those labels don't mean so much here, not in the local picture," Vasto said. He leaned back, his hands behind his head. "Yeh, Russ Dobson was our state senator. Two terms. He had the lumbermen in his corner, and that's the power here. He had it all his own way, maybe for too long. He got careless, right? A couple of shaky deals he gained from personally; a little high-handed sometimes; tricky personal life—a chaser, right? He started staying in Sacramento too much, forgot to come home and mend fences, especially with the lumbermen. When they favor a man, they expect him to show up at their wing-dings, be seen around them, show the flag."

"He had a bad reputation with women? A bachelor?"

"A reputation. How bad, who knows? This is whiskey

country, men are supposed to chase. But discreet, a weakness. Dobson got noticed." Vasto found a match, fired his black cigar in clouds of acrid smoke. "So, it adds up to maybe people can't be so sure of Dobson any more, right? Maybe he's too big for his hat, can't be counted on for something important."

Vasto leaned back, considered the ceiling. A soundproofed ceiling like the rest of the comfortable office with its heavy old furniture and small bar. Vasto saw me look at the bar.

"A drink? I've got the best. Private cellar."

He nodded to a locked door in the side wall.

"What was so important?" I said.

"Yeh," he said, smoking. "This ecology thing was important. The State Park redwoods, they're important. Does the state make it bigger, protect a lot more trees, or does the state reduce it, open up more acreage to the lumbermen? This is lumbering country, right? They want those trees. The ecology people want the Park—bigger and better. Important. The conservationists are pushing hard. The lumbermen needed a man to be sure of down in Sacramento.

"So they dumped Dobson in the primary, put up a new candidate. They own the party here, they could do it. A man they could be sure of all the way—Jesse Boetter: assemblyman, owns a trucking company, hates unions, thinks Governor Reagan's a little too liberal. No problems at the primary, Dobson was out."

"I saw his campaign posters in Grant's office."

"Did you see a party label?"

When I thought about it, I hadn't.

"Independent," Vasto said. "The lumbermen had the Republican ticket, and the Democrats made trouble of their own. They were taken over by the radicals. Real militants,

kids, antibusiness, down with lumbering. Nominated a
young guy used to teach college before he came back here
to turn his old man's farm into a kind of art colony and
organic experiment. Name's Tom Allen, a nice guy and
tough too. It gave Dobson his chance.

"He filed independent, campaigned with a lot of conservationist ideas, but also saw the good points of the lumbermen. A nice middle ground. He hammered his being
the incumbent with experience and connections. He played
on everyone's fears, our natural dislike of extremes and
natural love of the land. People are mixed up, Shaw, and
Dobson played them like a harp. Both parties had made a
mistake. Dobson got the more liberal businessmen, the
more conservative ecology people, and the practical people
who like the redwoods, don't much love big lumber, but
don't like too much state control and have to make a
living. He gave people somewhere to go besides right or
left, and he looked like a winner. Then—*boom*!"

Vasto was a good storyteller. I could almost hear that
explosion right in the office. Vasto seemed to hear it, too.

"Who?" he said. "No one can figure. The lumbermen
who'd dumped Dobson and knew they'd have a tiger by
the tail if he won? Or the radicals who were losing all their
moderate votes to Dobson? One side's power-hungry, the
other's violent. Take your choice."

"One or the other? It has to be?" I said.

"Who else?"

"An individual, maybe? Personal? An arrogant chaser
who made shady deals and feathered his own nest sometimes?"

Vasto thought about that. "Could be, I guess."

"It happened in your parking lot. Maybe you saw something, anything."

"Not a thing. No one here saw anything around that car."

"Her car," I said. "Why her car? He had his own, and you'd think a bomber would booby-trap his victim's own car."

Vasto chewed his cigar. "I don't know. That is sort of funny, right? How could anyone have been sure, right?"

"The sheriff say anything about that? *Her* car?"

"No, nothing."

"Was Dobson a regular in your place?"

"No. He spread his business around."

"Was Lillian Marsak his woman?"

"Not that I know. He'd dated her in the past, most men in Fort Smith with a few bucks had. Lillian got around. She ran a dress shop—manager, not owner—but mostly she ran after and with men with some money. She was a regular at my bar. Almost every night at five, like a homing pigeon."

"So if someone knew Dobson was seeing her around five-thirty, it would probably have been here. Her car would be here."

"Yeh, I guess so," Vasto agreed. "Someone had to know he was seeing her, right?"

"Why would Dobson go to her car, not his?"

"Could have been a lot of reasons. Maybe they were going to her place, he wouldn't want his car seen out front there. Or maybe he had a steadier woman he was hiding from."

"Someone would have to have known that, too," I said.

"Yeh, that looks so."

"Unless someone happened to overhear the two of them say they were taking her car. Maybe fifteen minutes ahead of time. Someone in your bar. Where were you, Vasto?"

He smiled. "I figured you'd get to that, right? No, I was here in my office with four solid citizens. A meeting. That's one reason I wanted to see you, to head you off before you got ideas about me because it happened in my lot."

"What's another reason?"

"I said I had a stake in it. Politics. I like to know what's happening, and I like having it all straight. You're going to dig, I want it open where I stand up here."

"Where do you stand? Which side?"

"No side, not now. You see, I was behind Dobson. He was my choice, even with some money. I lost my candidate, too. You understand?" Vasto found and lit another of his twisted black cigars. "That's why I told you about all I own—this place, a hotel, a lake lodge, tourist businesses. I didn't mention a big part of Dobson's looking like a winner—the tourist business. There are a lot of us who make our living from this being a resort area, and we like the State Park and the redwoods. They bring the tourists. We decided Dobson was our best bet, even if we didn't much like his methods. Now we've lost him."

I nodded. "And you wouldn't bomb your own man."

"No."

"That's what you wanted me to know."

Vasto puffed on his black cigar, let the cloud of dark smoke drift up around his head. "It happened here, you were investigating, you're an out-of-towner. I figured The Pines would be maybe your first stop, you'd be thinking about me pretty soon. I just saved you some time."

It could be the truth, he'd analyzed me right. I had been on my way to The Pines. He'd saved me time, explained that he had no political motive for killing Russell Dobson, and it could be checked out. Only perhaps Dobson's killing hadn't been political. If it hadn't been, Vasto could be

laying a smoke screen as thick as his cigar smoke. I didn't
say that.

I said, "Okay, time saved. Do I thank you now?"

"I thank you," Vasto said. "Now how about that steak?"

"Why not," I said.

10

THERE WAS STILL some last light when I parked on San Mateo Lane. A nice quiet street of big houses but not mansions. Upper-middle-class, with large front lawns and hedges but not a lot of land around each. On a hill, with a good view of both the sea and the distant Coast Range inland, was a yellow stucco two-story house, carrying the number 27, which belonged more in Southern California. Two blackened chimneys and storm windows showed that we were in the north.

A gardener, still mowing the lawn next door, watched me walk up to the entrance. So did someone at a curtained window in the house on the other side. Number 27 itself was dark, closed up, as if trying to hide the shame of having had its owner murdered. A motherly older woman with narrow, unmotherly eyes opened the door. She wore an apron over an old dress, and her hands did work. A housekeeper or cook.

"Yes?" Her voice matched her eyes—narrow.

"My name is Shaw. I'm a detective working for Campbell Grant on Senator Dobson's murder. I'd like to ask—"

"No, you're not," she snapped. "He fired you."

She slammed the door. I had my hand on the button to ring again, damn her, when I sensed the car behind me. It was moving very slowly down the quiet street in the last light. A sheriff's car. The driver was watching me. I didn't have much choice. Campbell Grant had passed the word, and the unmotherly type would turn me over in an instant. I didn't want to spend my first night in jail. I walked back toward my car.

"Mr. Shaw!"

She stood in the opened doorway of number 27, two steps out in the twilight. A tall, slender woman in a green suit. I went up the walk again. The sheriff's car stopped on the street.

"Come inside," the tall woman said.

She waved to the sheriff's car. It drove off slowly, almost reluctantly. The tall woman followed me inside. We were in a small carpeted entry hall hung with no less than four mirrors and paintings of Western scenes in massive gilt frames. Russell Dobson had liked Western pictures, gold frames and himself.

The older woman in the apron came into the hall. "Miss Cathcart, Mr. Grant fired this man."

"I'm not interested in what Campbell Grant does," the tall woman said.

"Nosy outsiders are—"

"We'll have some coffee in the study, Mrs. Sarguis."

Mrs. Sarguis walked stiffly out of the hall.

"In here, Mr. Shaw," the tall woman, Miss Cathcart, said.

It was a leather-and-law-book study hung with impressive-looking diplomas. The tall woman sat behind an ornate gilt desk. I took a fat leather armchair that sighed as I sat down. I waited, but Miss Cathcart said nothing for a time. At least five feet ten, she had the crisp manner of a lady judge, but wasn't thirty yet if I was any expert, and her slender look came more from her height than from being thin. She wasn't thin at all, no. Big bones and a good figure. Her breasts filled the green suit jacket, and her smooth face had no hollows. Her dark hair just touched her shoulders, neat but not severe. She seemed to study me while I studied her.

"I was his executive assistant," she said. "A glorified secretary, but glorified is better than not glorified."

Her smile was small, and her voice, when it came, was low and strong but just a little shaky.

"For a long time, Miss Cathcart?"

"Five years."

"You liked him?"

"Sometimes," she said. "You're here to find out who killed him, Mr. Shaw? And why?"

"Mostly who. I don't much care about why."

"I do," she said. "Everyone assumes it was politics. I want to know."

"You don't think it was politics?"

Before she could answer, the older woman in the apron, Mrs. Sarguis, came in with the coffee in a silver pot on a silver tray with bone-china cups. She left without pouring. Miss Cathcart poured. She took it black. So did I. She stirred her coffee too much.

"You're young, Mr. Shaw. You don't look like a private detective."

"I'm older than you, and our suits don't always bulge with guns and pints of whiskey," I said.

"Not very much older than I am, and I've met private detectives before. Rough, practical men mostly. Policemen."

"I wanted to be an actor. I studied. Maybe it shows."

"Why did you change?"

"I wasn't good enough."

She was silent. "Most people wouldn't admit that."

"Maybe not," I said. "Why don't you think Senator Dobson's murder was politics?"

"No." Miss Cathcart shook her head. "I didn't say that. It probably was politics, but what kind? Personal politics by one man who wanted to win, or a group plot to eliminate the voters' choice, or even an attempt to discredit the whole election. Was it calculated or was it fanatical? Is it a conscious attempt to control this county, or an act of irrational idealism? Was it Russ Dobson himself or what he was standing for?"

"Does it matter, Miss Cathcart?"

"It matters to me." She stirred her coffee. "Do you have a cigarette?"

I gave her a cigarette, lit it. Her voice still shook: "The Cathcarts are an old family here. Four generations. I'm the last. We're independent people, Mr. Shaw. I'm not fond of large governments or of making bigger and bigger state parks, but I'm not in love with today's kind of lumberman, either, or the tourist trade here. I love the trees, this land, but I don't like radicals who would destroy our ways under the cover of saving the trees. That's why I went to work for Russ Dobson, and that's why I influenced him to run as an independent against the lumbermen and the radicals. Now he's dead. I want to know what forces are really at work in this county. My county!"

There was more than a little passion in her speech. There was even a kind of fanaticism. The free-lance fanaticism that opposed everyone in some way. A Patrick Henry kind of fanatic who, in the last analysis, trusts no one to think or act right and true except himself.

"Four generations out here is a long time," I said. "How did the Cathcarts succeed, make their money?"

"Lumber. There were enough trees then, too many."

The old story. The Cathcarts made their pile in lumber, and now, in the fourth generation, got ecology-religion. But what they really had wasn't a sudden belief in the sanctity of the land, now that their pile was made, but a sense of ownership. It was *their* land. They had grown rich enough on the spoils, and now it must remain untouched. No one else must despoil it, no sir. It was their land.

"Was Senator Dobson seeing a lot of Lillian Marsak?"

"No!" Sudden, and her voice became stiff. "At least, I don't think he was seeing her."

"Who was he seeing?"

"I couldn't say. There was someone, yes, but there always was with Russ. Here and in Sacramento." Some bitterness?

"He was a woman-chaser?"

"Some people would say so."

"What do you say?"

"I don't."

"He never married?"

"No."

"Did he chase you?"

"That's insulting, Mr. Shaw."

"Why?" I said. "He was a good-looking, respected bachelor."

She was even stiffer, like some puppet, and her smooth face seemed to be paler. "Yes, I suppose he was. I liked him as a man, yes. But there was never any romance, and it was the implication of office high jinks I found insulting."

"Sorry," I said. "All right, you don't think he was seeing Lillian Marsak regularly. Did you know he was meeting her at The Pines that evening?"

"No."

"He must have been on a busy, tight schedule campaigning so near election day. Can you detail his schedule for that day?"

"Yes, I can. The sheriff wanted it, of course, so I wrote it up from the appointment book, and I remember it. Perhaps you should make notes."

I got out my notebook. She stubbed out her cigarette.

"At seven A.M. that Monday he had a conference with Campbell Grant at our office. At nine he had to speak at a Lions Club breakfast. Before he left for the breakfast his sister, Cynthia, came in and they had a rather heated argument. About what I don't know. They never agreed on much, even though they were a great deal alike."

"His only brother or sister?"

"Yes. Cynthia is fifteen years younger: twenty-five. She doesn't live here, has her own place in town."

"Go on."

"At ten A.M. he had a radio debate with the Republican candidate, Jesse Boetter. At eleven he addressed a chapter meeting of the Daughters of the Golden West. He lunched at his Athletic Club with Tom Allen, the Democratic candidate. He—"

"Lunch at his club with his radical opponent? Why?"

"He didn't say." Her voice was holding back.

"Was it usual for Dobson to have lunch, alone, with his rivals? A private lunch?"

"No, it wasn't."

It was there again, something unsaid in her voice. I let it pass for now. Whatever it was, I wouldn't hear it unless she wanted me to. Or unless I found out some other way.

"After lunch?"

"Two brief speeches from our sound truck in tract sections, and at three he met with Sam MacGruder, head of the Lumbermen's Association. MacGruder had called earlier, the senator had canceled an afternoon conference with Campbell Grant. I don't know what time he left MacGruder's office, but that was his last appointment until nine o'clock that night, when he was to speak at a Chamber of Commerce dinner.''

"That's a pretty busy day.''

"Normal for a candidate near election, Mr. Shaw.''

"Did he come back to the office after MacGruder?''

"No. I never heard from him again until they called me to say he was dead.'' Her voice shook again, but she didn't flinch.

"Did he often stop at The Pines for a drink?''

"No. He usually stopped somewhere about five o'clock, but nowhere regularly. To show himself to the citizens, talk.''

"He said nothing about meeting Lillian Marsak? Not even to let you know where he'd be?''

"Nothing. I'm not—'' She stopped.

"You're not what?''

She chewed her lip. "I'm not surprised he didn't tell me. Lillian Marsak is well known in Fort Smith, and not for her brilliant conversation.''

I suppose there's some bitch in every woman. It could mean nothing, but Miss Cathcart was more than a little uptight about Russell Dobson's sex life. Maybe only the office-wife syndrome, the proprietary habit of most secretaries.

"About nine months ago Dobson got a letter from Los Angeles. Marked 'Personal,' return address: 148 Ashford Way. Remember it?''

She was silent. A full minute. "Who told you that?''

"Campbell Grant.''

"He had no right!'' That shaky voice. "It was private business with an old friend who needed help. Russ told me. He said he was obligated, went down to L.A. for a day. That was all.''

"What friend?''

"Someone from the Army. I gathered it was a financial problem. Russ settled it, and that was all. Campbell Grant had no call to even mention it.''

"You don't like Grant, do you?''

"No. He came here only a year ago. To be a big fish in a smaller pond. He worked for politicians in San Francisco, was recommended to Russ when we wanted a new campaign manager. But the only man he campaigns for is himself.''

"You resented him?'' I said.

"Perhaps,'' she said. She became silent for a moment. "Mr. Shaw, Campbell Grant is a major reason why I want to know what happened to Russ Dobson. I want to be in a position to assess what Grant is up to. I think he might try to take Russ's place, run himself.'' She looked at me. "That could be why he wants you off the whole case.''

"A deal? The murder goes unsolved, he gets backing?''

"It's possible, Mr. Shaw.''

"Then maybe I better find out. How do I meet the others? Jesse Boetter, Tom Allen? How do I meet the sister?''

She hesitated. That "something" being held back again.

"All right, I can help you.''

11

THE BONFIRE BLAZED high up the rocky beach. Steep cliffs rose behind the beach, and it was ringed by jagged rocks that towered like castles in the night. Out in the sea, three giant rocks jutted out of the white surf, monsters in the flickering light of the bonfire. As we approached through the sand, figures moved around the bonfire like ancient savages in some ritual dance at the mouth of a cave.

"Beach party?" I said. "Who do I meet here?"

"A political meeting. But they're here on the beach a lot, anyway."

"They?"

"You wondered why the senator would have a private lunch with his opponent. Now you'll find out."

I heard it in her voice—distaste. A tightness again, as if whatever she had brought me to see was something that offended her somewhere inside, repelled her. Maybe it was just the scene as we reached the big fire. Half-naked bodies glistening in the firelight even in October; bearded men with long hair; loose-haired young women whose breasts moved free under their blouses, who wore tight pants or bikinis; some guitars; everyone staring into the flames, talking softly and easily.

There seemed, at first, to be no center to the groups, no focus. Then, as the young people around the fire glanced up at us lazily, I sensed a vague flow of attention toward where the largest single group sat and lay on the sand around a short, muscular young man who looked like a lifeguard. Naked to the waist, wearing only a pair of battered blue jeans, without shoes and his hair long but not very long—acceptable hair, the length and cut worn today even by young lawyers and executives. Not that young, I discovered when I looked more closely. Late twenties, or even close to thirty. A strikingly pretty girl sat beside him.

Miss Cathcart walked up to the young man. She had taken off her shoes, carried them to walk in the sand. The young man smiled up at her.

"Come to join the radicals, Nancy?" he said. He glanced at me—a shrewd, appraising glance. "With a friend, too?"

"This is Mr. Paul Shaw, Tom," Nancy Cathcart said. Whatever it was she didn't like, the young man was part of it. The radical young Democratic candidate—Tom Allen.

"Shaw?" Allen said. "So he's the L.A. detective I've been hearing about? I thought Campbell Grant fired you?"

"It didn't take," I said. "How do you know so much about me, Mr. Allen?"

"Call me Tom," Allen grinned. "Fort Smith is a small city."

"How long have you known that Grant hired me? From the start? When he hired us?"

"Since you showed up here and he fired you." Tom Allen had stopped grinning. "He told Cynthia right away, of course. He figured you'd go to her about her brother's murder, right?"

Allen nodded toward the striking girl beside him. In her

tight, flared corduroy slacks and a purple blouse she appeared small, but had those full hips and large breasts of so many slim young girls today. She didn't look much like her dead brother's picture on the posters. She was thin-faced, with large eyes and soft full lips, and looked younger than her twenty-five years.

"Are you going to find out who killed my brother?" she said.

"Yes," I said. "I am. Do you want me to?"

Because I had the picture. Why Russell Dobson had eaten a private lunch with Tom Allen. Not with the opposing candidate, but with his sister's boyfriend. That was what Nancy Cathcart had been holding back, and what she didn't like much. Cynthia Dobson had had a violent argument with her brother early that day.

"Don't you think I want my brother's murderer caught?" the sister said.

Tom Allen said, "He thinks maybe we killed Russ, Cyn."

"Did you?"

Cynthia Dobson moved closer to Allen, held his arm. She watched me and Nancy Cathcart. Whatever Nancy Cathcart felt about the sister, Cynthia returned in spades from her look. Tom Allen seemed to be studying the dark night outside the fire, and the rough sea beyond where the rocks towered.

"I've come to this beach most of my life," the young candidate said. "In the day you can see the mountains and the redwoods all around. At night there are the rocks and the sound of the surf. Every year it changes, becomes less. If the lumbermen have their way, it will all vanish. No more beach like this, no more redwoods, no more eagles. I might murder to stop that, maybe I will someday, but we didn't kill Russ Dobson."

"Because he was backing conservationist ideas?" I said. "You think he really believed what he said? Would work for conservation?"

"Hell, no. Not for a second. Maybe he'd have done something for the State Park just to get even with the lumber boys for dumping him, but that's all," Allen said.

"My brother believed in being senator, period," Cynthia Dobson said. "The beginning and end of his beliefs."

"But killing him wouldn't have helped us," Tom Allen said. "This isn't a beach party, it's a political meeting— our way. We've been talking about our chances. They never were much, but with Russ Dobson dead they're zero. Even if they don't believe we did it, the town's against us now—the wild, violent radicals. Pull-back time, all Jesse Boetter and his right-wingers. Not that the lumbermen were ever worried, not really. Unless, of course, you can prove Boetter's people bombed the car."

"If that was true," Cynthia Dobson said, "the city would just find a good law-and-order man in the middle to elect."

"Like Campbell Grant?" I said.

"The Dobson mantle?" Tom Allen said. "You know, I wouldn't be surprised. For a stranger, you see the situation nicely."

"It's the situation all over," I said. "You had lunch with Dobson the day he died, Allen. What about?"

"Me," Cynthia Dobson said. "What else? Russ always—"

"Easy, baby," Allen said, watching me. "Dobson didn't like me going with Cyn, I'm not his type. But that wasn't what we talked about at lunch that Monday."

"What did you talk about?"

"The redwoods. I knew he was going to win in November. I never stopped trying to get him to take a more extreme position in favor of the park, get him to promise to really back the park extension in Sacramento. I'm a dreamer."

"What did Dobson say?"

"He said he'd give it a lot of thought, but he was smiling when he said it."

Tom Allen laughed in the night wind and surf. Nancy Cathcart glared at him, the late Senator Dobson's tall assistant angry in the hot firelight.

"Russ Dobson would have done more for the redwoods and this whole country than you ever will!" she said.

Allen nodded. "That's possible, Nancy. Not because Dobson would have done much, but because no one will listen to me."

"My brother was an immoral destroyer!" Cynthia Dobson said. "He had no principles, no ethics! A playboy, gambler and liar! He and my father ruined my life until I met Tom!"

"Take it easy, baby," Tom Allen said again.

I said, "What do you two know of his relationship with Lillian Marsak?"

"Nothing," Tom Allen said.

"He used to know her, but I thought he dumped her as he dumped every other woman," Cynthia Dobson said.

"Did either of you know he was meeting Lillian Marsak?"

"No," Allen said.

"Could his murder have been something besides politics?"

A total silence fell on the people around the bonfire. I hadn't been aware that they were all listening until then. The other young people had seemed to be busy with their own actions, their own thoughts. But they heard my question, and for a time none of them said anything.

Allen spoke at last: "With Russ Dobson anything is possible."

"Any ideas, Allen? Miss Dobson?"

"No," Cynthia Dobson said. "We weren't close."

Tom Allen shook his head. No one else around that circle of fire offered anything. Nancy Cathcart seemed to be watching them as closely as I was. If Dobson's tall secretary saw anything, her face didn't show it.

"You plan to go on with your campaign?" I said to Allen.

"We'll go on," Allen said, "even if Dobson's people put up a new candidate. We're young. Someday we'll win. By growing to be old and the only ones left, if no other way."

"When you grow old, maybe you won't be the same," I said.

"Maybe not," Tom Allen agreed.

He didn't believe that. When you're young you never do. It all seems so possible and important when you're young. I was only a few years older than Tom Allen, but already, for me, not much seemed possible, and even less seemed important. Maybe it was my profession, seeing men stripped naked inside so often.

I left the bonfire and the beach with Nancy Cathcart and a sense of loss. I wondered how long they would be young? How long their beach and rocks would be clean and unspoiled?

12

IN MY CAR above the rocky beach, the distant bonfire light flickering on our faces, I watched Nancy Cathcart.

"Something on your mind?" I said.

She didn't answer me at once. Her fine face was fixed out toward the ocean through my windshield, her eyes large and staring as if the shadowy rocks tall in the sea were dragons she had heard about but had never expected to see. She still watched the dark waves when she spoke: "Russ Dobson would never have said he would think about any suggestions Tom Allen had, never! Not even at a private lunch. He'd refused to discuss the State Park with Allen. I heard him tell Allen that once to his face. They'd gone over it all long before, in private and in public."

"Then what did they have lunch to talk about?"

"I don't know."

I felt her shiver. She moved against me—a few inches, no more. The night was growing very cold and chill near the sea. Maybe that's all it was. Or had she thought of the same thing I had?

"Cynthia Dobson suggested that they talked about her. Her and Allen," I said. "Allen stopped her talking—twice."

She nodded, shivered again, leaned against me. "Paul, when I said maybe it wasn't politics, I was only half serious. I meant that perhaps it wasn't ordinary politics, perhaps it was some one man's attempt to steal power. Now—"

"Cynthia Dobson and Tom Allen, Nancy? What about them?"

"I'm not sure. I mean that. They've been engaged for over a year. That's not like young lovers these days, is it?"

"It could be. Are they living together?"

"I think so." That stiffness in her voice again. I was beginning to understand it—men and sex. "But not openly. Cynthia has her own place. They're careful."

"That isn't like lovers today," I said. "Not getting married, yes, maybe, but hiding? Why? And why engaged? An official engagement?"

"Yes, and they were hiding, I suppose, because Russ Dobson didn't approve. He didn't think Tom Allen right or good for her."

"What could he do? She's twenty-five."

"I think there's something about money."

"Money? An inheritance?"

"Her inheritance, I think. Russ Dobson said something once about his father being a tough, smart old man, and Cynthia was finding that out. It seemed to amuse him."

"He was fifteen years older than Cynthia?"

"Yes."

"When did their father die?"

"A long time ago. At least twelve years."

"So Dobson would have been twenty-eight, and Cynthia only thirteen. Dobson would probably have been her legal guardian. The question is, What hold did he still have on her now?''

Nancy Cathcart seemed to think for a time. ''She hated Russ, but she never left Fort Smith when she came back from college. She moved out of the house, but she came often to the office. They weren't close, but they saw each other frequently.''

''A pattern of some hold,'' I said. ''Something tying them together maybe against her will. Do you know anything about their father's will?''

''Only that there was quite a lot of money, and Russ Dobson didn't get it all.''

''I'll check it out. Meanwhile, Allen claims that Dobson's death hurt his chances in the end. Is that true?''

''I'd say so, yes. It's made people scared and angry.''

''And scared people pull back, go conservative. What about this Jesse Boetter and the lumber interests? Helped?''

''Yes. The voters have nowhere else to go.''

''Unless someone like Campbell Grant gives them somewhere. Would the lumbermen be in trouble then?''

''I can't say, Paul. Perhaps. Wash their hands of both sides, the voters. But it's awfully late.''

''Yes,'' I said. ''I'll take you home.''

I drove slowly out of the beach parking area, and the night seemed to move. To my left the shadows of the tall trees moved. I watched my rear-view mirror. A car was behind me, coming as slowly as I was, its lights out. Silent as the shadow it had seemed like parked under the trees unseen. How long had it been there?

I reached the county highway, turned toward town. The car followed me, switched on its lights as it came onto the highway and passed under a highway lamp at the entrance to the beach parking lot. A sheriff's car. A second one? It made no attempt to overtake me. I didn't try to lose it. I watched it in my rear-view mirror. There was something about it, the shape. I wasn't at all sure it was the same car that had first come out of the shadows of the trees. The sheriff watching me—and someone else?

Nancy Cathcart lived on Pimiento Lane, not too far from San Mateo Lane. The same upper-middle-class area. Not as big a house as Dobson's, but not small, and older, with the reserved class of long residence, and when I pulled up in front of the house the sheriff's car was no longer behind me.

"You live here alone?" I asked.

"Yes. I was born here. Where else would I live?"

There was something stiff about the big old house, as there was about Nancy Cathcart herself.

"You'll be here tomorrow?" I said.

"I'll be at the senator's office or house. We're winding up his affairs. There's a lot to be done."

"I'll find you if I need you," I said.

She hesitated a moment, and then she smiled at me before turning up the walk to her door. It was a good smile, soft and yet strong. She was a solid woman, attractive and self-controlled, but she had her problems. Somehow, I sensed that Russell Dobson had been one of them.

13

YOU SENSE WHEN you're being followed.

All the way back to the Redwood Inn I didn't see a sheriff's car behind me, and yet I sensed someone back there. It was barely ten o'clock, the traffic heavy enough in Fort Smith, and I couldn't spot anyone behind me—yet I sensed it.

I parked in front of my unit and went up to the second-level outside corridor. I didn't go in. I waited in the dark where the balcony-corridor turned to the rear. After a few minutes an old car turned slowly into the parking area, went past my car, turned at the far end and came to a stop where it could see my car and unit. A battered Ford, at least ten years old.

It sat there doing nothing. No one got in or out, but I saw a shadow behind the steering wheel, and then the flare of a match and the drifting smoke of a cigarette. I didn't think this car was from the sheriff's office. Neither were the two killers down at the motel in Bodega Bay—or I didn't think they had been, you never knew.

Too many people were interested in me.

I slipped around to the rear and went down the outside stairs. I circled the unit and came out on the far side behind the old car and across the parking lot from it. There was no way to reach it under cover. I got out my stubby Colt and walked toward the car.

Its engine suddenly started. He'd seen me. I began to run at him. For an instant I had the sensation of running very fast, terribly fast, the old car jumping closer. Too fast—he was in reverse and backing straight at me! My brain flashed—a panic mistake, or was he trying to run me down? A flash, no more. No time to think. I had thought too long, was still running toward the car that came backing at me in a squeal of tires. I flung myself sideways and down.

Something hit my right ankle like a sledge hammer, turned me around in midair, sprawled me skidding on the macadam of the parking lot. My face had skinned blood. I heard a shattering crash as the old car backed straight into a wall behind me. I tried to get up.

The car came off the wall and at me again, going in forward this time.

I dived down again, rolled, and the car went on past me and didn't stop. Before I was up, it had turned on the street with its tires screeching and vanished.

I stood shaking.

Then I checked.

My face was scraped raw on one cheek, my left wrist hurt where I'd landed on it. My suit was torn on one sleeve and all up the right pants leg. My right ankle hurt like fire, but it wasn't broken. A small gash and a big bruise tomorrow, that was all.

No one came out of any unit or the office to look. Tires squealed all night in motel parking lots. I limped up to the second-floor balcony-corridor and went into my room. I tossed my pistol onto the bed, got the telephone book. I called Tom Allen's home number first. No answer. I called the number listed for Cynthia Dobson. No answer. Swell!

I called room service, ordered a double Johnnie Walker Black and soda, lit a cigarette, and called Campbell Grant's home.

No answer.

I called the number listed for Jesse Boetter. A clipped-voiced woman answered. I asked for Boetter. His voice was all smiles and the glad-hand. At least he was home.

"Mr. Boetter, I'm Paul Shaw. I'd like to talk to you."

"Shaw? I don't know—"

"About Senator Dobson's murder. I'm a det—"

"Yes, now I know. I don't want to talk to you."

He hung up hard.

There was no home number listed for Sam MacGruder. The office of the Lumbermen's Association would be closed, but I tried it, anyway. It was closed. That shot my bolt. There was no point to calling Salvatore Vasto. If he was at his roadhouse or not would prove nothing—he had too many men who worked for him.

My drink came. I drank it, smoked, and none of the calls meant much. Those not at home could be anywhere, those at home could have hired a man to watch me, attack me. All the calls had done was cool my anger, make me feel I was doing something. What? Learning that any one of them could want me out of town or out of this world? I knew that already from Delaney and Bodega Bay. Or did I?

There was something clumsy, amateurish, even inept about the man in the old car down in the parking lot. I'd spotted him easily, he'd tried to run me down in a kind of panic, like a crazed-with-fear bull. The one who had shot

Delaney had done a clean, sure job, and the two in Bodega Bay had acted like professionals.

Not the same party behind all? It opened up the angles. The pros could be politics. The clumsy one tonight could be more personal. Both?

My ankle was like numb fire. Something torn or badly bruised. I sent out a call for another Scotch double, called Mildred in Los Angeles.

"They operate tomorrow, Paul."

"He hasn't said anything?"

"He said something," Mildred said. "That he hurt. He came out of the coma today. He said he saw one man, black. Campbell Grant said Dobson had gotten a letter from the Ashford Way address, that was all. He passed out again."

"What do the doctors say?"

"That Dick has a good chance tomorrow."

"I'll keep in touch," I said.

I thought of calling Maureen, she should be at home in our penthouse her money paid for. But the Scotch came, and somehow I didn't feel like calling Maureen. It happens. I didn't want to talk to my wife tonight so far away. I was angry, and I hurt, and the Scotch was getting to me, and I was thinking of tomorrow.

Or was I thinking about Nancy Cathcart? I hadn't called her, but she knew more than anyone where I was going after I left her. I was thinking too much about her. Tall and stiff and with problems. A challenge?

I went to bed.

14

BOETTER & COMPANY, TRUCKING, was a complex of busy garages and warehouses on the southern outskirts of Fort Smith. I could see in the distance where the redwoods started along the coast. The tall trees, packed in masses with their incredibly straight trunks towering almost out of sight, were enough to make a good lumberman's mouth water.

The office of Boetter & Company was on the second floor of the main garage where the smell of grease and oil could reach like incense to a trucker. There was no receptionist. A hurrying clerk directed me to the rear where a dirty glass door was stenciled: JESSE BOETTER, PRIVATE. I went in. Two men were talking; one behind a littered desk, the other standing in a corner chewing something. The one at the desk looked up at me as I closed the door behind me.

"What is it?" he snapped, interrupted.

"I'm looking for Jesse Boetter."

"Okay," he said.

He was a nondescript man of medium size with a small

belly covered by a well-cut brown suit, and a round,
flabby face of the kind you can see by the thousands at any
sales convention. The salesman's perpetual fixed smile
under eyes that didn't smile much, the soft flesh that never
saw the outdoors but tried to stay reasonably in shape, a
kind of formlessness to the face. A thin, determined mouth.
The kind of man who had worked hard all his life with
neither much time nor interest for thinking of anything
except work and his own success at it.

"I'm Paul Shaw," I said. "You hung up on me last
night. But we're going to talk about Russell Dobson now."

"You should have taken the hint," Jesse Boetter said,
leaned back in his chair. "Get out of here."

"I can get the police."

"No, I'll get them, mister. I've already talked to the
police, and that's the last talking. Who's your client, eh?"

"Nancy Cathcart."

"Bull!" Boetter leaned forward across his desk, a finger
like a gun at me. "You don't come in here and push any
weight at me, mister. I don't care if you've picked up a
new client. I've got the weight here and in Sacramento.
You better just crawl back to L.A. with the rest of those
L.A. creeps."

"Do you need weight, Boetter? From what I hear, you
stand to gain most from Dobson's sudden elimination. I
expect most of your mechanics know how to plant a bomb
in a car."

"Me!?" He was up behind that desk. A little taller than
I had thought, but not much. "Out of this office!"

The man in the corner said, "Hold it, Jess."

"I don't have to take this crap," Boetter said.

"We'll hear him out, Jess," the man in the corner said.

He wasn't exceptionally tall, the man in the corner,
about six feet even, but he was broad in a suit that looked

too small for him. Bald, with a big wind-leathered face, he wore a Western shirt and a lanyard string tie, and his boots were muddy. He looked like a rich rancher, but his hands were too clean, and in this county it wasn't the ranchers who were rich and had the power. I could almost smell sawdust on him.

"You hear him out in your office," Jesse Boetter said. The trucker looked flabby, but he didn't back down easily.

"We'll both hear him," the broad man said. "It's better."

"Don't tell me what I'll hear!"

"I'm telling you," the broad man said.

At another time, in another age, they would both have had their hands on their sword hilts by now. Heavy, medieval swords at their sides. Two feudal barons facing each other in quick-tempered pride. Hunters grown into barons with the fierce pride of action and status. Each a lord, each with the same pride, but one just a degree less strong, a half a step lower in the system. Jesse Boetter wasn't a man who backed down easily, no, but he backed down. The broad man had the half step.

"Then hear him, damn it," Boetter said, sat down again, a fury in his eyes.

If he had disliked me before, he hated me now. I had seen him bent by a bigger baron, and if this had been feudal days I wouldn't have wanted to fall into his dungeons. The broad man didn't seem to notice Boetter's anger, the incident forgotten already. He could afford to forget it, he had won.

"Sit down, Shaw," he said. "I'm Sam MacGruder. You probably want to talk to me too."

It wasn't exactly a surprise. MacGruder would be the power here. I sat down. Sam MacGruder didn't. He leaned against the filing cabinet in his corner.

"I head the Lumbermen's Association, but you know that. Just what do you expect to learn from us you don't know?"

"I'm trying to learn who killed Russell Dobson."

"What do you think we'll tell you about that?"

"You never know what a man will tell you, even if he doesn't mean to."

MacGruder shook his head. "I could tell you Jesse there planted the bomb, or I did, it wouldn't mean a damn. You'd have to prove it, and you're not proving anything in Fort Smith. You think if I bombed a man I'd leave proof, anyone who'd talk?"

"You own the whole town? Everyone in it? I'd say no."

"You're an outsider, Shaw. Leave it to the sheriff."

"No," I said.

It was my turn to face-off sword to sword. No baron, the knight-errant, the quest. Robin Hood against the Duke. Speed and the longbow against armor.

"It's a hard way to make money," MacGruder said.

"My partner was shot, might die yet."

His wind-squinted eyes narrowed, his face changed a little. He understood the necessities of an injured partner.

"We didn't have your partner shot, Shaw. We didn't bomb Russ Dobson. We didn't have to. We dumped him for good reason, we weren't worried. We don't murder. Talk to those radicals."

"I did. They say they only lost ground by the murder. If anyone gained, you did."

"I don't know if anyone gained. It's my job to see that we don't lose if it can be fixed any way."

"No wasting good trees on tourists, MacGruder? No matter what has to be done? That's how I read you."

"The trees are money, Shaw. Money is the story. For

everyone. People count, and business is where people live.''

"If Dobson won, you don't get your trees.''

"We get them. Even if Tom Allen won, we get them in the end.''

"I wonder,'' I said. "You met with Dobson at three P.M. that day. Why? About what?''

"Politics. That's all you get.''

"You knew he was meeting Lillian Marsak around five?''

"Why would I?''

I looked at Jesse Boetter. "How about you, Boetter?''

The trucker didn't answer me. He made a nasty noise.

"Where did he go from your office, MacGruder?'' I asked. "At what time did he leave that Monday?''

"He left about four-thirty, I don't know where he went,'' MacGruder said. "He had a telephone call, and he left.''

"A call from who?''

"He didn't tell me.''

"You have a switchboard in your office?''

"No.''

"But you must have taken the call first. No name? No identification by the caller? A man or a woman?''

"A woman. No on all the rest.''

"Would you happen to know Lillian Marsak's voice, MacGruder? I hear she was popular with the rich men in town.''

The office atmosphere had been cool, now it froze. Sam MacGruder watched me as if I were some insect in his lumber. Jesse Boetter sat up. I had felt the animosity all along, now I felt a lot more—danger.

"I didn't know Miss Marsak,'' Sam MacGruder said coldly.

Jesse Boetter said, "He's going to dig dirt, Sam. You hear? His kind are all the same. He'll smear us, Sam.''

"No, he won't," MacGruder said, leaned against that filing cabinet like the feudal lord considering just how hard to hit a potential threat.

"Where were you two between four-thirty and six o'clock that Monday?" I said. "Maybe you did recognize Lillian Marsak's voice, MacGruder. Maybe you followed Dobson to The Pines. Maybe you called Boetter there, and he went to The Pines."

Jesse Boetter said, "He's going to smear, Sam."

"Yes," Sam MacGruder said.

"Someone planted that bomb," I said. "Someone shot my partner, tried to shoot me. Someone doesn't want outsiders looking for who planted that bomb."

Jesse Boetter said, "Accidents happen in garages, Sam."

"Yes," MacGruder said. "You've got men who'll do a job for you, Jesse? Men who keep quiet?"

"I've got the men," Boetter said.

"Okay," MacGruder said.

I reached into my jacket for my Colt in its holster. Sam MacGruder moved fast for a big man. He had my arm. He was very strong. More than half again my age, over fifty, but his fingers were like his own logs. I hit him in the stomach. He grunted, doubled over, but didn't let go. Jesse Boetter came around his desk fast.

The outer door opened.

"Hold it right there, Jesse. Let him go, MacGruder."

He walked into the office. A small, slim man in a sports jacket and gray slacks. A bow tie on an ordinary white shirt. The face of a clerk or small real estate man, and the manner of a not-so-successful small real estate man. A reluctant manner, like someone forcing himself to do what he wasn't sure he wanted to do. He was unarmed, but Jesse Boetter and MacGruder backed away from me at once. Boetter sat down again.

"He threatened us, Frank," MacGruder said.

"I heard some of it," the small man said. "He was asking questions."

"We don't like cheap parasites asking us questions, Sheriff," Jesse Boetter said.

"Maybe not," the sheriff said, "but I don't like private strong-arm tactics. Next time just tell him to leave. Okay?"

"We asked," Boetter said. "He wouldn't go. We've got a right to—"

"No, Jesse, you don't. You've got a right to call me. That's the job you elected me to do."

"Is it a good job, Frank?" Sam MacGruder said.

"I can do without it, Sam. Any time. I'm not in love with it. But as long as I've got it, I'll do it. Shaw has a right here. Remember that, okay?"

His voice was mild, even conciliatory, but I could see that he was a man who meant what he said, would do what he had to. MacGruder and Boetter seemed to know that, too. He was an ordinary man, but he was the sheriff.

"Keep him in line then, Frank," MacGruder said.

"I will. Come on, Shaw."

He made it sound like a suggestion, a request, but it was an order. I followed him out.

15

His CAR WAS unmarked, a black Ford. We sat in it in front of the warehouse. I saw Boetter at his office window, and the truckdrivers stared at us as they worked. The sheriff didn't seem to notice them. It wasn't an act. He had those nerves that are unconcerned with, even unaware of, what isn't immediately important to the work in hand.

"Campbell Grant tells me he fired you," he said.

"Nancy Cathcart hired me." It was a lie, but I thought the tall assistant to Dobson would back me if asked.

"Then that's all right," the sheriff said. He lit a cigarette, gave me one. "My name's Quigley. Frank Quigley. Three years ago I had a small real estate agency and law practice. Ten years ago I was an FBI agent. I got my law degree at night, I like security, and I owe the lumbermen a lot. My main job is to keep the county secure, give honest men a chance to work in safety. I'd rather let a criminal have a way out than corner him and force him to make trouble here."

He looked out toward the distant redwoods, and toward a column of smoke rising into the high blue sky from a nearby lumbermill. "But I try to run an honest, fair county. I try to protect trees and business. I don't like the radicals, and I don't like the arrogance and muscle of the big lumbermen, and I don't like the con games some of the tourist-traders and real estate men try to run here. I've been watching you."

"I know."

That didn't bother Quigley. "The way you've worked says you think the bombing was political."

"Don't you, Sheriff?"

"Maybe. Tom Allen lost support by it, and I can't believe Sam MacGruder would have to resort to anything like that. It looks like they've gained by it, but this is a county of rugged individualists. They're talking of running a new man in Dobson's place. If it's too late for that, there's talk of boycotting the polls and running a recall campaign against whoever wins. MacGruder knows this county too well to think he could gain much by bombing Dobson."

"What new man would they run in Dobson's place?"

"They're even talking about me," Sheriff Quigley said.

"Campbell Grant?"

"It's possible."

"Maybe there's a motive—personal politics. Not a matter of sides, but of an ambitious man who wanted Dobson gone."

"Campbell Grant's got an alibi, and so do I." The sheriff didn't smile. "Too chancy—bombing a man on just the hope of taking his place."

"Unless someone had more than hope," I said. "But you think there was a personal motive? Simple murder?"

"Dobson was a sharp dealer and a chaser," Quigley said. "Only, he cheated no one in this town, and I haven't found any wives or sweethearts he was mixed with. Around here men don't murder over women, they beat up the other man, fight."

"A jealous woman? Because he was with Lillian Marsak?"

"Dobson had a steady woman. Single, not the jealous type, and as far as I can tell, that Monday was Dobson's first time with Lillian Marsak in over two years."

"Some jealous man?"

"Same answer. Dobson couldn't have been serious about her."

"A woman you don't know? Such as Nancy Cathcart?"

Sheriff Quigley thought. "She might have liked Dobson that way once," he said, "but not for a couple of years. Formal as hell with him, reserved, no dates. Old family, Shaw. A cool one."

We both thought. I could still see Jesse Boetter up at his window. I didn't see Sam MacGruder. The truckers watched us, and Quigley watched the mill smoke drift over the redwoods like some omen.

"Sheriff?" I said. "Dobson was killed in *her* car. You don't seem to think that's odd at all. Why?"

The sheriff lit another cigarette. "We had a man guarding Dobson. It was his idea, claimed danger from outside radicals and right-wingers. Made a public show of it to pull more votes from both extremes, we figured, but we gave them all a man."

"You mean *his* car was being watched by police?"

"Car, apartment, office. Our man followed him around. Not at his side. None of them wanted that."

"But that made it hard to plant anything in *his* car, so you weren't surprised that it was her car that blew up."

Quigley nodded. "A bomb has to be made. That takes time and a plan. We figure the killer made his bomb, waited until he found a good chance. It bothers me some that the killer was so sure Dobson would be in her car, not his, but I guess he'd heard something sure, found out somehow.''

"What about relatives, Sheriff?''

"He only had one.''

"I know,'' I said.

The sheriff smoked, watched the redwoods off in the sun. "You know your work, do it fast. Anything to tell me, maybe?''

"No, just a hunch. The day he died Dobson had lunch with Tom Allen. Allen says they discussed something Nancy Cathcart says Dobson wouldn't have discussed, so Allen could be lying. Everyone says Cynthia Dobson and her brother didn't get along, she says so, too, and yet she seemed to be tied to him, and was in his office that morning arguing. As if he had a hold on her.''

"Money,'' Quigley said. "Their old man was a hard character, domineering male. When he died Cynthia was still a kid, so he named Russell guardian and trustee of her money. It's a pretty good fortune by now, I hear, and the old man threw a curve. He stipulated that she couldn't have her money free until she was thirty unless she married someone Russell Dobson approved. The old man didn't think much of women.''

"Do she and Tom Allen need money?''

"Need, no,'' the sheriff said, "but they want it. They want to turn that place of Allen's into a study center—ecological and political. They have big plans for saving the world.''

"They both saw Dobson that day, could have known about Lillian Marsak and The Pines.''

"They had a meeting arranged with Dobson for six-thirty that evening, too. They claim he called it off, but they can't account for their time from five-thirty until seven.

They say they were waiting for Dobson. No one saw them."

I said, "You like them as suspects, don't you?"

"Right now they're my favorites, yes," Sheriff Quigley said. "Only, I can't prove anything. My lab tells me the bomb was dynamite, get it anywhere. Most of the wiring was old. The trigger mechanism was old—army issue. Only the fuse cap was maybe new, bought somewhere. A common cap, but I'm trying to find everywhere around that sells them. Otherwise, I've got nothing. No clues, no witnesses."

"Maybe I can dig something up."

Quigley nodded. "I could use any help, Shaw. We're not a big department, and we're not so well equipped for this kind of investigation. A good man, experienced, is what I need."

"I'll do my best."

"Thanks. I hoped you would. Only remember something, Shaw. My main job isn't solving a murder, it's running a quiet county. Don't play it too loose or rough, or I'd have to stop you."

16

NANCY CATHCART WAS sitting on the stairs up to the balcony outside my room at the Redwood Inn. She had changed today to a sky-blue blouse and shorter dark-blue skirt that fitted her hips. A much shorter skirt. She had very nice legs. Her dark hair was pulled back and tied at the neck. It suited her height better, softened her stiffness.

"I hear you're working for me," she said, stood up.

"Am I?" I said. "Lunch hour, or just a break?"

"Lunch, but I came to you first."

"Then lunch is on me," I said. "Who called you? Sheriff?"

"Sam MacGruder. I said you were working for me. Was I right saying that?"

"Very right. I'm supposed to have a client."

"Did you find out anything from Sam MacGruder?"

"Only that he doesn't like me around, doesn't want trouble, and that Dobson got a call from a woman in his office that Monday. It wasn't you who called, was it?"

"No."

"Was he in trouble over a woman? Recently?"

"Trouble? No, not that I know," she said. "Can we have that lunch? I have to get back."

Was it automatic with her, the cold water? The direct, stiff statement that seemed to cut short any warmth toward her? Hurt by some man? Or raised by an old family who thought no man could be good enough for her? Or had I said something, asked the wrong question?

"Then we'll eat right here," I said.

The restaurant at the Redwood Inn was good. A pleasant atmosphere, and a good crabmeat salad. That is something a detective has to live with—that he enjoys himself, eats, smiles, even makes love, while in his mind is someone who will never do any of those things again. Life has to go on. Not insensitive, a matter of simple survival, sanity. So I ate, smiled and told her about my morning. She was intent on my whole story, frowning over it, but I sensed her watching me, too. Seeing my face, hearing my voice, as much as my words. I felt that challenge—a cool one, reserved, the sheriff had said. But I had her interest in more than one way. I knew that much.

"Cynthia and Tom?" she said. "I can't believe that."

"Dobson didn't approve of Tom Allen. Did they want money?"

She stirred her coffee. "They were always talking about Tom's plans for a study center, a third-way institute here."

"Allen was probably lying about his meeting with Dobson that day. They were anxious to marry. Can you remember anything about them that day?"

"No. I didn't know Russell was going to meet them."

"Maybe he wasn't," I said. "A cover-up story. Or maybe he was going to meet them at The Pines."

She shook her head. "Paul, I won't believe it. You must be wrong. Not Cynthia."

"I'm often wrong."

"No." She looked up at me. "No, I don't think you are."

"Cynthia hated Dobson, didn't she, Nancy?"

"Yes, I think she did," she said. "You're not often wrong, are you? Because you don't lie, or cheat, or hurt people to get what you want."

"Everyone hurts someone," I said. "There's almost nothing you can do or want that won't hurt someone. What I get, someone else can't get. Every winner has a loser."

"Honest, yes, but not cruel," she said, her voice almost fierce. "Hurt sometimes, you have to, but not use."

"Are we talking about something, Nancy?" I said.

"What?" Her eyes were wide, distant. "You. We're talking about you, I think. And Cynthia Dobson."

"How do I find out what she's been doing, Nancy?"

"Her friends, perhaps. The beach people. Her friends at her apartment. Not all the beach people like Cynthia and Tom. The Democratic party workers, perhaps."

"Let's go then," I said.

She waited at the door while I paid. Tall and almost beautiful today. Was that me? That's something few men can resist—the feeling that for them a woman has become more beautiful. I took her arm as we went out and across the parking lot to where I had parked my car in front of my unit.

The legs stuck out from under my car.

Legs of a man that protruded from under the front end of my company car moved as if the man lay on his back working on something over his head—working on the underside of my motor.

"Nancy, walk away from me. Now. Behind the unit. Wait behind the corner."

She had seen the legs. She didn't shrink or make a sound. That old-family aristocratic control. She watched me take out my gun, and then walked back to the corner of the motel unit. Only when she got there did she look back. I motioned her to go behind cover. She vanished, but I knew she was still watching. No violet, no. Calmer, surer, less volatile than Maureen.

The legs continued to move, the man working hard and fast under my car. Thin legs in bright-green slacks with green socks and green suede shoes. I stood over them, my gun out.

"Come out," I said.

The legs stopped moving for a moment, then went on, the man under the car working again.

"You under the car. I said out. Hands in sight, empty."

The voice was muffled. "Back off. I've almost got it."

"Out! Right now."

"Take it easy, for God's sake," the muffled voice said.

The legs seemed to twitch, and I heard a low exclamation. The legs began to come out. Slowly, carefully, the man working out on his back. He came into view—the little terrier in the loud clothes who worked for Salvatore Vasto: Jack Ready.

"Stand—" I began, and stopped.

Resting on the little man's chest, held there by both his hands, was a compact object of wires, circuits, clamps and six sticks of dynamite. Jack Ready stood up very slowly, holding the bomb in front of him. "Saw this guy around your heap," he said calmly. "Ran when he spotted me. I had a hunch, you know?"

"The field," I said. "Over there behind the motel."

We walked through the parking lot and past the last unit toward the open field behind the Redwood Inn. Ready carried the bomb like eggs, firmly but gingerly.

"Saw bits of wire around on the ground," he explained as we walked, his eyes steady on the bomb in his hands.

"So I crawled under. You never know. Maybe a time bomb, a bad job could go off and hurt someone."

"What man did you see?"

"Too far when I spotted him. Average-looking guy, in a windbreaker. Never saw his face. Ran away from me. So I crawled under and there it was. Clamped tight. Broad daylight. Who notices a man under a car? Some mechanic, right?"

"Where did he run to?"

"A car."

"Old Ford? Beat up?"

"Chevy, I think. Pretty new."

Ready told it all quietly, even blandly, but both our minds were on the bomb in his hands. It shouldn't go off, but even I could see it was a homemade job, and amateurs make mistakes. Ready's story could be true, or it could be all a smooth cover-up for a man caught in the act of planting a bomb on my car in broad daylight.

We reached the field.

"Set it out in the center," I said.

Ready walked out to the center of the field, laid the bomb down, walked back without haste. Then we both stood there looking back at it for a time. Ready lit a cigarette. So did I. Nancy Cathcart stood behind us near the Redwood Inn. She began to walk up.

"You can't identify the man who planted it?" I said.

"Not a prayer," Ready said. "Lucky I happened to just see him."

"Lucky," I said.

We smoked. The bomb sat out there in the field like some sacred idol we couldn't take our eyes from. Nancy Cathcart stood beside me.

"I called the sheriff," she said. "It was for you?"

"Yes," I said.

"Nothing but pieces," Jack Ready said. "It went off, it was all nothing but pieces. Six sticks. Damn!"

"Why were you here, Ready?" I said.

"Came to get you again," the terrier man said, smoked, watched the bomb. "Vasto wants to see you. He's got something for you."

"What?"

"He didn't tell me."

The sheriff's sirens wailed up at the motel. Quigley came toward the field with two deputies and a man in a heavy padded suit. The deputies took positions behind us. Quigley and the bomb man stood with us.

"Ready saw a man, average, no face, driving a new Chevy," I said.

"What were you doing here, Ready?" Sheriff Quigley asked.

"Mr. Vasto sent me to get Shaw."

Quigley looked toward the bomb with us. "It looks like the same type again. Homemade, dynamite, old wire."

"Yes," I said.

"Daylight at a motel," Quigley said. "Crazy."

None of us were looking at the bomb man in his protective suit. He hadn't said anything, just studied the bomb out there in the field.

"What do you think, Diaz?" Quigley said to the bomb man.

"Looks simple. I'll see."

He walked out. As if on a simple stroll, but there had been sweat on his face. He knew his job, I supposed, but each bomb was individual, each time could be the one that went wrong. He earned his pay. In the field he kneeled down, seemed to study every small piece of wire without touching anything for a long time. Then I saw him nod, take out a small screwdriver from his suit, bend close to the bomb.

My cigarette burned my fingers in the warm sun.

Traffic rolled behind us on the road in front of the Redwood Inn.

Out in the field the bomb man, Diaz, stood up.

"That's it," Sheriff Quigley said. "We'll work it over, but I don't expect to learn much."

"No," I said.

Nancy Cathcart said, "I better get back to the office. Will I see you later?"

"I'll call."

"All right."

Sheriff Quigley said, "We'll get statements at my office."

The bomb man, Diaz, brought the bomb.

17

IT WAS MIDAFTERNOON when Jack Ready and I walked into
The Pines roadhouse. Salvatore Vasto had a woman in his
office with him.

"This is Della Kurtz, Shaw," the roadhouse owner
said. "She was Russ Dobson's woman."

She was a handsome woman, not young. Maybe forty,
heavy but not fat, with gray streaks in her hair. A solid
woman with an intelligent face, and soft, resigned eyes. A
comfortable woman, I sensed, who had seen enough of
trouble and complication in her life to want only a peaceful
existence, and some corner with some man who would
treat her well enough. She wouldn't demand a lot, no, and
wouldn't want too much demand placed on her.

"Miss Kurtz," I said.

"Mrs. Kurtz," she said in a nice, rich voice. "I'm a
widow, Mr. Shaw."

Salvatore Vasto smiled at the woman from his desk
chair. His easygoing manner had an alertness to it this
time, more than a little interest in Della Kurtz. With his
sweater off in the warm afternoon, a better blue suit on, he

cut a more handsome figure. Della Kurtz had no man now,
and she could do worse. Vasto looked like he had the same
idea. Jack Ready had taken a chair against the wall, showed
no interest in anyone. The big, slow man with the silver
star in his lapel, Ben Wheeler, stood next to Ready, almost
touching the smaller man as if he had to have support.

"Did you know Dobson was seeing Lillian Marsak,
Mrs. Kurtz?" I said.

She smiled. "He wasn't. One night, and he never even
got that, did he? Poor Russ. I wasn't jealous, Mr. Shaw, if
you have that in mind. I wouldn't know how to make a
bomb. We had a good 'arrangement,' Russ and I. No
problems, no obligations. He helped me out, you know,
and I was there when he needed me. A good system, male
to female. He gave me money, I didn't have other men.
Beyond that, it was just two people who liked each other.
He was busy, away a lot, I never asked where or what."

"Has the sheriff talked to you?"

"Frank Quigley? Yes, he talked to me. I'm not in it."

"Vasto wanted us to talk for some reason."

Salvatore Vasto said, "Tell him, Della."

"Someone was blackmailing Russ Dobson over me,"
the widow said. She shrugged, shook her head as if she
didn't understand people. "Fort Smith is a funny place.
I'm from L.A., things are different there. Up here men
chase after women every day, but they're not supposed to
be caught at it. Like the Old South in books. Men chased
other men's wives all the time, but if they were spotted
they had to leave town even if the husband did nothing.
Matter of honor."

Vasto said, "We all knew Dobson was a chaser, right?
Only not publicly. We knew, but we didn't see, right? The
town knows in private, that's not so bad, but if it comes
out in the open in public, then we're supposed to do

something, right? A man lets people *see*, that the town don't take."

"The Puritan hypocrisy," I said. "It figures."

"People knew about me and Russ," Della Kurtz said, "but we never showed in public. We kept it quiet, private, never out together in Fort Smith. It's happening, but you pretend it isn't. You don't challenge the good people, you hide. But someone was putting pressure on Russ by threatening to make our relationship public. That would have hurt him in Fort Smith."

"Make it public how?"

"Something about a morals charge. Publicity that would have to bring us out."

"Who?"

"I don't know that. Someone close to Russ, though. With Russ running independent, he was worried it could hurt him a lot around this time."

"It could have," Salvatore Vasto said, "but blackmail isn't so good around here, either, right? If it was one of the other candidates, Dobson would maybe fight back."

Or maybe the blackmail hadn't been all political. Some pressure for a private reason.

"How long had you and Dobson been together, Mrs. Kurtz?"

"Off and on maybe three years. No strings, though."

"Does the address 148 Ashford Way mean anything to you? That's in Pacific Palisades."

"No," she said.

"He got a letter from there about nine months ago."

"I never saw any letter. Nine months, you say?" Mrs. Kurtz thought. "Russ went down to L.A. for a day or so around then, some old buddy in trouble. Maybe a year ago he was down in L.A. for almost a month on business. He called me a few times that month. I remember because

Sacramento was in session, and Russ didn't usually do private business then.''

''A year ago? Where did he stay in L.A.?''

''I didn't ask, Mr. Shaw.''

Vasto said, ''Dobson was always going somewhere on business. Being a senator don't pay enough to keep them from handling their own business every chance they get, right?''

He was right, yes, but a whole month away from the legislature when it was in session was a long time.

18

JACK READY AND his giant shadow, Ben Wheeler, were at the bar of The Pines. I joined them. Ordered a bottle of beer.

"Lucky you came to my motel today," I said. "Another five minutes, I'd have been in the car."

"Sometimes you need luck," Jack Ready said.

"Funny you had such a bad look at the man near my car."

"I was too far away then," Ready said, drank his beer. "No way of knowing the guy I saw was the bomber, anyway."

"You and Wheeler there are together a lot it seems. Old friends?"

The massive Wheeler said, "Me 'n' Jack been together a lot o' years, right, Jack? All the way from the Army, yeh."

"A lot of years, Ben," Ready said.

"Jack he got me the job with Mr. Vasto," Wheeler said, almost proudly. "Like he got the brains, I got the muscles. That's right, ain't it, Jack?"

"You've got enough brains, Ben," Ready said, drank again. "When you use them. Come on, we've got work."

Ready finished his beer. Ben Wheeler gulped at his. It was almost full as if he'd forgotten he had it.

"But Wheeler wasn't with you today at my motel," I said.

"He was busy," Jack Ready said.

"Cleanin' out Mr. Vasto's private cellar all mornin'," Ben Wheeler said. "All mornin' I was workin'."

"You're both around The Pines most of the time?"

"In and out," Jack Ready said. He watched his big partner drinking his beer. Impatient.

"Senator Dobson wasn't as lucky as I was," I said. "Were both of you here that Monday?"

"We were here," Ready said.

"You didn't happen to hear Dobson say anything?"

"No," Ready said.

"We wasn't in the bar, you know?" Ben Wheeler said. "We was down the cellar, right, Jack? Both of us was down there."

"That's right, Ben," Ready said. "Finish that damn beer!"

"Sure, Jack," Wheeler said, drank. "We was down the cellar, 'n' we heard that *boom* real loud. They was dead right off, you know? *Boom!* Senator 'n' her. We seen the senator when we run up."

"You spend a lot of time in the cellar," I said.

Ready said, "It's part of his job, Shaw. What the hell do you want sucking around us?"

"I'm trying to understand how the bomber knew that Dobson would go from here to Lillian Marsak's car. Did he talk about it in here? Did someone overhear in time to plant the bomb? Who else was in the bar here that night?"

"I don't remember," Jack Ready said. "I wasn't in the

bar, right? Not long, anyway. Maybe he'd told someone he was going in Lillian's car. He wouldn't go to her place in his car. Not in this town, not him.''

"How do you know he was going to her place?"

"Where else would they go?" Ready said, laughing.

Ben Wheeler finished his beer. "Everyone goes to her place. All the time, yeh.''

"Let's go, Ben,'' Jack Ready said.

I finished my beer.

19

CAMPBELL GRANT'S RECEPTIONIST told me he was out on a coffee break. I found him in a greasy-spoon diner a block away having a bear-claw Danish with his coffee.

"So you're still around," Grant said.

"Nancy Cathcart hired me." I sat down facing him.

He bit his bear-claw as if he hated it. "The frigid bitch."

"How do you know? Did you try her?"

"I tried," Grant said. "What else do you do in this benighted hole?"

"Did Dobson try for her?"

"Not while I was here," he said, chewed his Danish. "What do you want, Shaw? I told you there'd be no help from me."

"Why? Why don't you want me around?"

"The sheriff will do the job. I said that already."

"Did you know Dobson was meeting Lillian Marsak at The Pines that night?"

"No, I didn't know that."

"He canceled a conference with you to meet MacGruder. Maybe you went looking for him, found him at The Pines."

"No, I didn't. Damn it, you're spoiling my coffee!"

"Nancy Cathcart thinks you maybe hope you can take Dobson's place. A new plan. That's why you fired us."

"Does she really?"

"So do Tom Allen and the sheriff. They say you could be nominated in Dobson's place. Now or later. Maybe after a recall campaign against the winner this time. Jesse Boetter, probably."

Grant finished his coffee. "I didn't come up here to carry Dobson's sword forever. A few years, get to know the city, then work for myself. It just happened sooner. Yes, I'd run for the office now or later if I can get it. Why not?"

"Have you got a promise? From the lumbermen? From Vasto and his tourist interests? Try to hush up the murder in return for backing?"

"Nothing says I had to go out of my way to find out who bombed Dobson, and I can accept any support I choose."

"A lot says you can't make the opportunity by getting rid of Dobson. One way or the other."

Grant stood, dropped fifty cents on the table. "You might make me mad, if you didn't make me laugh."

"Did you know Dobson was being blackmailed?"

"Blackmailed? Over what?"

"His steady woman, Mrs. Della Kurtz. By someone who knew him well; like you, Grant. Maybe to make him quit the race?"

"I knew nothing about Dobson and his floozies!"

He stalked out of the diner.

I had a cup of coffee.

20

THE SHERIFF'S OFFICE in Fort Smith was in the old brick courthouse, first floor rear with the entrance on the side. Quigley was behind his desk in a small one-window office. I closed the door to shut out the noise of the deputies working in the big main room.

"Della Kurtz says Dobson was being blackmailed."

I sat down across the desk from Quigley. The sheriff lit a cigarette. I saw that his fingers were heavily stained with nicotine. A man who smoked too much. It was the job. He looked like a small businessman who has just lost a good customer.

"One of my deputies talked to her twice," he said. "He never found that out. You're sure?"

"I'm sure, she says so."

"They'll never give me the budget to get a decent job done here. I'm a necessary evil, but they don't want this office too powerful. What was it for? Money, politics?"

"One or both, or maybe private pressure."

"Who?"

"Mrs. Kurtz doesn't know. Someone close to him, she thinks."

"How did they figure to do it?"

"Some kind of threat to bring a morals charge in public."

"That'd have hurt him. All over the papers," Quigley said. He thought. "We do have some old laws no one's used in fifty years. It wouldn't have stuck, the county prosecutor wouldn't have touched it, but there would have been a field day. Who do you think?"

"I talked to Campbell Grant. He just about admitted he was in a deal with someone for political backing. He denied any blackmail, but it's the kind of trick he might have tried to force Dobson to resign the race in his favor."

"If Dobson wouldn't play, fought back, Grant just might have had to kill him. His alibi is good, but maybe not perfect. He was at his house on the beach waiting for a friend who never showed. Witnesses say he was there, but he could have maybe slipped out, and anyway, he could have hired the job. But why would he go down and hire you people then?"

"Maybe he felt safe, wanted to look good. Delaney could have found out something, called him to tell him. So he shot Delaney, then fired us so I wouldn't find out anything."

"I don't know," Quigley said. "Tom Allen? He had Cynthia Dobson in his corner, she was close enough to Dobson."

"Or MacGruder and Boetter."

"No, that I can't see," Quigley said. He smoked in the small office, thought for a time. "There wasn't any unusual money missing from Dobson's bank accounts, we checked that. In fact, he'd made some pretty big deposits recently that we could find nothing to explain."

"Deposits? During a campaign?"

"Yeh," Quigley said. "Funny, isn't it?"

"A man doesn't usually make money during a campaign."

"No, he doesn't. Let's take a walk."

We walked across the main street to an old two-story building directly facing the courthouse. Quigley went up to a second-floor office marked LUMBERMEN'S ASSOCIATION. Three women worked at desks in a rustic outer office. A giant wall map had the whole northern part of California marked off in colored sections to show the lumber holdings of each company. The women barely glanced up as we walked through to the rear office. They weren't interested in the sheriff.

Sam MacGruder was alone in the private office. He didn't get up when he saw us. He nodded to Quigley and looked at me, then went on with some paper work he'd been doing. Quigley sat down and waited. I stood against a wall. After a few minutes Sam MacGruder pushed his papers away, smiled at the sheriff.

"What can I do for you, Frank?"

"I don't mix much in state politics or lumbermen's business, do I, Sam?" Quigley said.

"That sounds like you're about to," MacGruder said. "Does it concern Shaw there?"

"This time it does," the sheriff said. "I never thought you or Jesse Boetter would bomb Dobson, not for political angles, anyway. Personal, maybe, but not for politics."

"I'm glad of that, Frank. So?"

"So I didn't think so because I couldn't figure you or the lumbermen having to bomb anyone to get what you wanted. I couldn't see you really taking the risk of losing any ground in Sacramento. The lumbermen don't leave their interests to the voters if they can help it."

"Practical politics," MacGruder said.

"I saw that someone had paid Dobson good money during the campaign. I said nothing about it, it wasn't my business. Now it is. Your association was paying Dobson, Sam."

MacGruder said nothing, swiveled slowly in his chair.

"You don't take chances," Quigley said. "Dobson had always been your man. You dumped him, he fought back, and it looked like he might win. That would be bad for you. You had a candidate, but two candidates are better than one. I expect you'd have bought Tom Allen too, if you could."

"We tried," MacGruder said blandly, swiveling in his chair. "We gave up on Allen after Dobson started taking votes from him. Okay, sure, we were paying Dobson. No real secret. He agreed with our stand, really. He was only using that ecology crap for votes, anyway. So we had a talk, agreed to kiss and make up. In private. We still wanted Jesse Boetter to win. Dobson was too independent, but we wanted to make sure Dobson would play our side mostly in case Boetter lost to him."

I said, "No matter who wins, the lumbermen win."

"That's right, son," MacGruder said. "Now you know."

"A lesson in practicality. Only a naïve fool would think you had to bomb a man to win an election."

MacGruder smiled thinly. "You said it, I didn't."

"Shaw is from the big city," Quigley said. "Thanks, Sam."

"Yeh," Sam MacGruder said.

I followed the sheriff out. There was no point asking Sam MacGruder about blackmail. The lumbermen wouldn't have to use blackmail on a man like Russell Dobson any more than they would have had to use a bomb. We crossed back to the courthouse.

"I'll put a man on the blackmail," Quigley said. "Della Kurtz might be able to tell him something that would mean more to us than to you. With Dobson dead, I'm not optimistic."

"No," I said. "The bomb on my car tell you anything?"

"Only that the cap was the same type, probably bought at the same place. It'll help if we have a real suspect."

"When we have a suspect, we won't need it."

"Yeh, that's the way it usually works," Quigley agreed.

I got my car, drove to a steakhouse for some dinner. While they were cooking the steak I called my motel. There was a message saying that Dick Delaney had survived the surgery, was doing pretty well, had said nothing more. I realized by now that Dick wasn't going to tell me anything further, I knew more than he did now.

Over my steak I thought about what Sam MacGruder had told. The lumbermen hadn't bombed Dobson, hadn't been blackmailing. That didn't rule out Jesse Boetter, he could have had a personal motive—he looked like a loser, and while that might not matter too much to the lumbermen, who took no chances, it might have mattered a lot to Boetter himself.

Then there was Tom Allen. The young radical was a loser once Russell Dobson got into the race as an independent and took a lot of the more conservative Democratic and conservationist votes. That might not have been so bad to Allen, as long as he believed that Russell Dobson would act on his conservation position. But what if Tom Allen had learned that Dobson was still really with the lumbermen all the way? What if Allen had found out that Dobson had taken the lumbermen's money and promised to return to MacGruder's fold? The extension of the redwood park would be almost doomed.

Then there was the blackmail.

21

CYNTHIA DOBSON'S APARTMENT was in a big old mansion in what had once been a good section of Fort Smith. The area was run-down now, a neighborhood of transients and the young. Tom Allen's jeep was parked in front. A guitar played somewhere in the night, and the big old house was bright with lights.

There was noise behind all the closed doors inside as I passed, youth in action. I knocked on Cynthia Dobson's second-floor door. The dead senator's slim, full-breasted sister opened the door. Her corduroy slacks were black this time, and her tight blouse gray, but her small face and large eyes were as antagonistic as the first time on the beach.

"It's the Sherlock Holmes," she said over her shoulder to the room behind, and to me, "Is it fun work?"

"It's work," I said. "Do I come in?"

Tom Allen spoke from in the room, "Let him in, Cyn."

She stepped aside, angry at me for just existing. I was an enemy. She had been raised to be first, to get what she wanted, to win at everything—as long as she remained a

woman in the world ruled by her father. She wanted to be
more than that, and raged now at the bigger world that
wouldn't give her what she wanted so easily, that didn't
care if she won or lost.

"What do you want, Shaw?" Tom Allen said.

He sat in a purple sling chair, next to a beer on a low
coffee table made from what looked like an African hide
shield. The new generation of leaders—blond and handsome like the last, but a long way from Madison Avenue
in denim work shirt and baggy old wool trousers and
sneakers. Not disdaining the material externals, the room
was nicely furnished in bizarre international, but not thinking about them, either. Our fathers had given him that
right by their work, and that was as it should be. Less than
five years between us, I knew, but I had wanted to be an
actor early, had a private dream, and that made a difference.

"What did you really talk to Russell Dobson about at
lunch the day he was killed?"

"You don't believe I wanted him to do more for
ecology?"

"I believe you wanted that, but you didn't talk about it.
There was no way to talk to him about that, and you know
it. Maybe you knew it even more that I thought."

"What does that mean?"

"That Russell Dobson was back in the pay of the lumbermen, was going to renege on even a mild conservation
position once he got elected. All fixed and cozy."

"You know that?"

"Yes. Did you?"

"God damn him!" Allen swore. He shook his head. "I
should have expected that, sure. That was Dobson."

"You're sure you didn't know it?"

"I didn't know it."

"Maybe Cynthia knew, told you? He was her brother."

Cynthia Dobson said, "Not so that anyone could notice. He wouldn't have told me his shirt size, and I returned the favor."

"Yet you were around him so much, stayed close," I said, turning to the girl. "How do you explain that? I mean, you're twenty-five, still you seemed to want his approval to marry."

They both watched me. I found a cigarette, lit it.

"How much money is it, Cynthia?" I said. "What your father left you that you don't get until you're thirty unless you marry someone your brother approved? You'll get it now, of course. More, too. His money, I expect."

It was Tom Allen who answered. "About a quarter of a million. Dobson was holding on to it. He didn't like me much, but I think he liked holding the money more."

"You wanted it?"

Cynthia Dobson said, "We wanted it. My money. My father believed women belonged under a male thumb. Russ had no right to stop me marrying Tom."

"But he was," I said. "No money for five years— unless he was out of the way. A political enemy, too."

"We didn't kill him," Tom Allen said. "That would have been pretty stupid. With our motives."

"Maybe, but a little blackmail wouldn't have been. Some private pressure. Your money for his political safety. That's what you talked about that Monday, wasn't it? A public morals charge that wouldn't stick, but would sure rock his boat."

They were both silent. I smoked.

"Some old moral law?" I said. "Never used, but on the books, and with plenty of nuisance value?"

"No," Cynthia Dobson said. "A civil suit charging that he wasn't morally fit to judge my marriage under the terms of my father's will. An immoral trustee."

"Better," I said. "That might actually have worked, and exposed him to public charge, too. Very good. It is what you talked about that Monday? Both of you?"

"Yes," Tom Allen said. "He asked for it."

"I'd say he did. What was his answer?"

"He never gave us a final one," Allen said. "At lunch that day he said he wanted to think. I gave him until that evening. But I think he was going to agree, let us get married. He was in a pretty good mood at lunch. He just wanted us to sweat."

"You were supposed to meet at six-thirty that evening?"

"Right here," Cynthia Dobson said. "He called it off at the last minute, said he'd see us in the morning."

"Last minute?" I said. "How?"

"Telephoned about ten to six," Tom Allen said. "Said that all of a sudden he had something better to do, had a chance too good to miss. A real juicy pickup. Damn skirt-chaser."

"Pickup?" I said. "He said he'd made a pickup?"

"His own words," Allen said. "A real juicy pickup. And *he* didn't approve of me for his sister!"

"A chance too good to miss?" I said. "An appointment to meet you two at six-thirty. He called it off at the last minute, just before six P.M. A pickup? You're sure, Allen?"

"That's what he told us," Tom Allen said. "Why?"

"It doesn't matter," I said.

But I was lying.

"I'll talk to you two again," I said, walked out of there.

If Allen had heard right that Monday evening, it mattered a hell of a lot—maybe.

22

THE HUMAN TENDENCY to miss the obvious, overlook the simple that stared us in the face? Our endless capacity to jump to the wrong conclusion because we see what we expect to see, make assumptions instead of really looking? If a king and a peasant are both shot by the same assassin, don't we automatically assume it was the king the assassin wanted to kill, not the peasant?

In The Pines I went straight to Salvatore Vasto's office. The massive muscle man, Ben Wheeler, lumbered to block my way from where he'd been sitting at a table near the rear corridor.

"I want to see Vasto," I said. "It's okay."

"You gotta wait here, okay?"

"I'm in a hurry, Wheeler."

"Sure, but Mr. Vasto says I don't let no one back 'less he says so. You just wait, okay?"

He vanished into the corridor. I lit a cigarette. The bar was crowded, and most of the restaurant tables were full at the dinner hour. Vasto had a good business. Ben Wheeler came lumbering back. He was smiling.

"Mr. Vasto says go on in."

I went on in. Vasto had his sweater back on now that it was night, but he wasn't as relaxed as he had been. An edge to his dark eyes. I didn't sit down.

"Who was at your bar when Dobson and Lillian Marsak were that Monday?"

"I don't know for sure; businessmen. The usual five-to-six drinkers. Mostly men, a few playgirls. Monday's slow."

"Tom Allen or Cynthia Dobson?"

"Hell, no. Never saw either of them in the place."

"Sam MacGruder? Jesse Boetter? Campbell Grant? Maybe Nancy Cathcart?"

"None of them, as far as I know. Most of them, I'd have been called so I could go out to the bar and say hello. I didn't go out."

"Who was on the bar that evening?"

"Same two men on now. You want to talk to them?"

"Just the one that served Lillian Marsak and Dobson."

"Sure." Vasto pressed a button under his desk. Almost at once Ben Wheeler appeared at the door. "Get the bartender who served Dobson and Lillian Marsak the day the bomb went off, Wheeler."

We waited. Vasto seemed to be absorbed in his own thoughts. He almost absently took out one of those twisted black cigars and lit it, blowing clouds of the heavy, acrid smoke. A man in a full-length white apron stood in the doorway. Vasto saw him after a moment.

"Come in, Marco," Vasto said. "Shaw here wants to ask you some questions about Lillian Marsak and Senator Dobson. You tell him straight, you hear? No tricks, I mean it."

The bartender, Marco, just looked at me.

"You knew Lillian Marsak pretty well?"

"She was a regular. Around five o'clock almost every day."

"And Senator Dobson?"

"Everyone knew the senator."

"Who came in first that evening?"

"She did. Lillian. Five on the dot."

"Did she say anything in particular?"

"She said a lot, she always did. Talked a streak. Who was doing what to who in town, and why."

"Anything about having a date that night?"

"Yeh. Like I told the sheriff, she checked her watch with me when she came in, said she had a date she sure didn't want to be late for."

Maybe I was wrong, or maybe Tom Allen hadn't heard right what Dobson had said on the telephone. Or maybe Russell Dobson liked to make himself seem sexier than he was.

"But she came into the bar alone?"

"No, she was with her friend, Ginny Piper. They came in together a lot of the time. Made contacts, you know?"

I knew. Would Lillian Marsak have come in with another woman if she had a date to meet Dobson?

"Then Dobson came in and joined her at the bar?"

"He came in later, yeh. Sat alone, though, for a while. Couple of stools away."

"They sat separately for a time? How long?"

Marco shook his head. "I don't know for sure. Ginny Piper joined a guy at a table; next I knew, Dobson and Lillian were together, he was buying her a drink. He made a telephone call."

"And at just before six they left together?"

"That's right. She was hurrying him some."

"Yes," I said. "Thanks, Marco."

Marco looked at Salvatore Vasto. The owner nodded,

and the bartender went out. Vasto smoked his twisted little cigar and watched me while I stood thinking.

"You got something on your mind, Shaw?"

"Yes."

Vasto studied his cigar, frowned. "I never heard Marco tell it that way before. No one asked him, I guess." He looked up at me. "They didn't have any date, did they? Lillian and Dobson. A pickup at the bar. That means someone had to be around here to know they were going out together to her car. That what you're thinking?"

"It's possible," I said. "Only, who was in the bar to hear? To see them? Someone with a bomb already made and in hand?"

"It doesn't sound reasonable," Vasto admitted. "But how else could it be?"

"I'll let you know if I find out," I said.

I went back out to the bar. Ben Wheeler waved to me from his table, and the bartender, Marco, watched me. I went to the telephone. A Virginia Piper was listed in the directory.

23

THE ADDRESS WHERE Virginia Piper lived was a good apartment court complex on one of the roads that led toward the shore. The Markham Arms. Small semidetached cottages around a grassy center court, with an archway over the central path. Her cottage was dark, no one answered my ringing.

I went back to my car, drove until I found a public telephone booth. I looked up Lillian Marsak. She was listed, too—at the same address as Virginia Piper. I drove back.

Lillian Marsak's cabin was two away from the Piper woman's. I circled it in the night. It was dark, too, and there was no police seal on the doors. Why would there be? Everyone had assumed she was only a mistake. I used my ring of keys on the back door and went inside.

There were two small rooms, a kitchen and a bathroom. The typical furniture of a decent furnished apartment, without any character, but comfortable enough. It was all neat and clean, the bed made in the bedroom, her clothes and make-up still there, but bunched and stacked as if

someone had taken inventory. The police, probably. They
had searched, too, Quigley was a thorough man. But they
wouldn't have been looking for the same things I was.

They would have been looking for connections to Russell Dobson. I was looking for Lillian Marsak's other
connections, whoever and whatever. Letters, a diary, notes,
clues to her life and any trouble that had been in it. I didn't
find much.

What letters there were came from her mother, post-
marked from a small rural community some fifteen miles
inland from Fort Smith. They were dull letters, cramped
and formal, but an uneasy love came through all the trivial
gossip and questions about how Lillian was, what she was
doing.

There was no diary, and nothing in the whole apartment
seemed to belong to any man. Matchbooks from what
seemed like half the bars in Fort Smith, random swizzle
sticks, postcards from traveling friends—all women or
couples.

There was no address book. Not anywhere. I looked in
all the drawers, in all her pockets and handbags. No
address book. It was the first pay dirt. I had never met a
woman who didn't have an address book. No man, either,
for that matter. The sheriff might have taken it, but I
doubted that. No, there should have been an address book,
and there wasn't. Someone had taken it.

The second, and last, possible pay dirt was in her top
bureau drawer. A pair of ruby earrings. I'm not an expert,
but I sensed that they were real. Real, and new. They
shined pristinely, and the gold glittered untarnished in any
way, unscratched or dulled. They were in a plain white
snap box, also clean, lined with satin but with no jeweler's
name anywhere. They were expensive, I was sure, and
they were new.

There was nothing else. After an hour I gave up and went out the way I had come in. I circled around to the front and Virginia Piper's cottage. It was still dark. No one answered my ring this time, either.

I lit a cigarette. I could wait or I could look somewhere else. Where? Lillian Marsak's parents lived too far away to go to at this hour, and Virginia Piper was my only other possible lead. I was tired, she could be out most of the night, and as I smoked there in the deserted court I saw a man watching me from the front. The manager's cottage. I left.

I was sure now, but was I? There were still problems. Until I had them worked out, one way or another, I didn't want to go to Sheriff Quigley.

But I had to talk it out to someone.

24

"IT WASN'T DOBSON, no," I said. "It was Lillian Marsak the bomber wanted dead. She was the target all the time."

She was in her robe and nightgown, Nancy Cathcart. A warm red and white floor-length gown with red ribbons at neck and wrists, and a voluminous red robe. We were in her living room. An old room, formal and dusty as if she barely lived in it. The whole big house not neglected but somehow deserted, lived in by one woman alone where once generations of a family had lived. She had made coffee.

"Then . . . Russ? It was—"

"An accident," I said. "Everyone just assumed the target had to be him. He was the public figure, the important man. He had no date with Lillian Marsak. A spur-of-the-moment pickup."

"Are you sure, Paul?"

"I'm as sure as I ever can be. Pure chance that Dobson was with Lillian Marsak in her car when it blew up. I always wondered about it happening in her car, about just how the killer could have been sure Dobson would be in her car that evening. The sheriff had a man tailing Dobson, so he assumed that the bomber couldn't get at Dobson in his own car. Just a piece of luck—chance, damn it.''

Nancy Cathcart sat prim in the big dusty room from another century. She sipped her coffee, seemed to huddle inside the gown and robe.

"Russ Dobson and his women," she said, her voice almost bitter. "No morals, not ever. Dead for a night—an hour—in some woman's bed."

"He paid pretty high for his flaw," I said.

She drank coffee. "I can't believe it, Paul. Not really."

"It explains a lot," I said. "No one seemed to really gain politically by Dobson's death. It was hard to see MacGruder risking murder, or Tom Allen stooping to it. Not for politics. Allen couldn't gain enough, and MacGruder and Boetter had safer ways to win what they wanted. The blackmail wasn't a killing matter, Dobson would have given in. We've found no jealous man or woman. No, Lillian Marsak was the target of that bomb.''

"Poor Russ," Nancy Cathcart said. "What do you do now?"

"Find out why someone wanted Lillian Marsak dead," I said, finished my coffee. It was good and warm. It made the old room warmer, made Nancy Cathcart seem soft and close in her nightclothes. "There are some things that still bother me, but I expect I'll find the answer now."

"What things, Paul?" she said. Did I hear a warmth now in her voice, too?

"That Pacific Palisades address for one. Going there was all Dick Delaney did, and then he got shot. A car might have tailed him from there. Probably the address means nothing, a coincidence, mere chance," I said. "But the way Delaney was shot, the way they tried to kill me down in Bodega Bay, is a different pattern from the bombing up here. I'd swear they were professionals, and the bombing looks amateurish—both the real one, and the attempt on me.''

''What do you think that means?''

''It could mean a lot of things. Maybe that there is one killer, and someone else who has something to hide and just doesn't want the investigation. Sometimes a murder like this, the chance death of Dobson, can open up a whole Pandora's box of other troubles.''

''Yes,'' Nancy Cathcart said. ''I suppose it can.''

She gave that shiver again where she sat wrapped in her warm nightgown and robe, her coffee cup empty now. Neither of us said anything for a time. Neither of us moved in that quiet old room of the big house where she lived alone. I felt that she was waiting, that it was time for me to move—to make some move toward her. The challenge.

''You said there was no romance between you and Dobson, no office high jinks,'' I said. ''But were you in love with him?''

''No.''

''Some people say you were interested in him once, a few years ago.''

''Perhaps I was a little, then. Before I knew.''

''Knew what?''

''About his women, what he did.''

''But you weren't jealous, Nancy?''

''No.''

''You don't like any man? Have a man now?''

''No.''

''Do you like me?''

''Yes.''

I stood up, went to her. She sat without moving, looked up at me. I bent and kissed her. Her lips were very soft, open. I picked her up. She lay against me in that silent old room. I kissed her again, harder. She shuddered.

She pushed me away—hard. "All of you. Every one of you!"

I stood back. "What is it? You want me, I know that."

"Want?" she said, her voice low. "Russ and his women. It killed him. Go away, Paul."

"Because I'm married?"

"No. Tonight? Then what? One night, two, three, and then alone in an empty house. Go away. Go!"

I went.

What did I feel? A fool? No, that's for boys. Cheated? I had no right. Sorry for her? Yes—male vanity. Guilty? Again? I suppose I always would feel that. There was a dark place inside me that would always reach into shadows.

I drove to the Redwood Inn and went to bed.

25

AFTER BREAKFAST I drove to Virginia Piper's apartment. In the bright cool morning the Markham Arms was a pleasant place. Two women talked in the center court over their strollers, the small children in the strollers eyeing each other. An old man worked in the narrow patch of garden in front of his cottage. A Mexican man was washing windows.

A young dark-haired brunette with an elegant figure and puffy eyes answered my ring at Virginia Piper's cottage. She wore a bright green silk wrapper, carried a piece of toast.

"Miss Piper?" I said.

"That's right," she smiled, appraised me. "Can I help you?"

"I hope so," I said. "May I come in?"

"Sure. A cup of coffee?"

"I'd like that."

Her cottage was the twin of Lillian Marsak's I had searched last night. The same anonymous furniture, but not as neat, the bed through the open bedroom door unmade. She sat me at the kitchen table—room for two and not much more—and poured me a cup of coffee before she sat down.

"Now, what is it, Mr.—?"

"Paul Shaw."

Her face closed up a shade. She knew my name.

"About Lillian Marsak," I said.

She drank coffee. "What about Lillian?"

"Who wanted to kill her, Ginny?"

"Lillian?" She shook her head. "You've got it wrong. It was Russ Dobson. Lil was just killed by accident."

"No. Dobson was killed by accident."

"Dobson?" She stared at me. "That's crazy. He had fifty enemies, who would want to kill Lillian? The sheriff—"

"The sheriff jumped to the wrong conclusion. Everyone did. Automatically, because Dobson was the public figure. But everyone was wrong. It was Lillian the killer wanted. You tell me why, Ginny, and who."

She was pale. "What makes you so sure?"

"Dobson wasn't Lillian's man, was he? They didn't date."

"No. She hadn't seen him for years, except around."

"But he was meeting her that night?"

"Yes, sure. He was in the car with her, wasn't he?"

"A planned meeting? A date? Made in advance?"

She blinked at me. "Well, she checked her watch, was going to meet someone. I . . . No, it couldn't have been."

"What couldn't have been?"

She shook her head slowly. "I never thought about it before. I mean, I was going to say she had some kind of date, so it had to be Russ Dobson, but it couldn't have been."

"Why not?"

"She wasn't happy about the date she had. I mean, it wasn't a 'date' exactly, I don't think. She didn't say, but I got the feeling it was some kind of business, something she had to do. And when Dobson came in, she sort of stared at him, waved to him. He sat a couple of stools away, and she waved like she was saying hello. He didn't come over right away. I had to make some calls; when I got back he was sitting with her, making a pitch."

"He picked her up, Ginny?"

"Yes, I guess he did."

"Then no one could have known he would be with her that evening. A bomb has to be made in advance. It takes planning to bomb someone in a car."

She nodded. "I never thought about it. I mean, that he picked her up. I just assumed—"

"Yes," I said. "So did everyone. But he picked her up on the spur of the moment, and no one could have known he would, so the bomb was meant for her, Ginny, not for him."

She was silent. Poured another cup of coffee for each of us without looking at the cups.

"She liked living so much, always on the go," Virginia Piper said. "Who would want to kill Lillian? Why?"

"That's what I came to ask you. Who were her men? Her enemies? Was she in any trouble, or having trouble with someone?"

"Men? God, she knew so many. Regulars and just some quick flings, too. She was never in any trouble I knew about. There were some guys chasing her, you know? Guys she'd dumped, and guys she'd never given a tumble, but she didn't tell me about anyone special giving her any trouble."

"Did she have a regular man recently?"

"Sure, she always did. Never knew Lillian to dump one man unless she had another."

"Who was he?"

"Walt Sobers. She was going with him about six months. He wasn't going to last with her, anyway."

"Why?"

"Truckdriver, works for Jesse Boetter. She was kind of hung up on him for a while, but no truckdriver would hold Lillian long. Going nowhere."

"You said 'anyway.' Was she breaking with this Sobers?"

"She had someone new on the string. I never knew who he was, but he was a real catch, she said. Maybe for a month or less before she got killed."

"That's all you can tell me? No other special men in her life from the past?"

"Maybe a lot, sure to be, but I don't know them."

"All right. Where does this Walt Sobers live?"

"Number 87 Modoc Street. It's on the south side."

"I'll find it. You wouldn't happen to know where Lillian's address book is, would you?"

"Address book? In her place, I guess."

"No."

"Then I don't know. It was always around on her bureau."

"Has anyone been in her place since she died? Besides the sheriff's men?"

"Not that I saw. I'm not home too much, though."

I thanked her.

26

NUMBER 87 MODOC Street was a two-story frame house on a shabby street not far from the lumbermills on the south edge of Fort Smith. Built like an army barrack with a flat roof, there were separate entrances to each floor, the second story reached by an outside stairway. W. Sobers lived on the second floor.

A shiny new two-door Buick with twin pipes, chrome and bucket seats sat in the driveway in front of the second-story steps. The license plate read WALT. I went up the stairs and rang the bell. A hi-fi played show music at full volume inside. I rang a second time, and the music went down. Heavy steps approached the door, and a man opened it.

"Yeh?"

"Can I talk to you, Mr. Sobers?"

The heavy step inside had fooled me. I'd expected a big, burly man—the truckdriver stereotype. He was short and dapper. Neither slender nor broad, an average welter-weight build, but with shoulders, and his clinging Ban-Lon shirt revealing a flat belly, slim waist and a body builder's muscles. His face was smooth and round, with a small mustache. His slacks were expensive. A man who spent his money and time on himself—cars, clothes, grooming and body building. He squinted at me.

"I know you," he said. "Yeh, somewhere."

"I don't think so," I said. "Can I come in?"

He didn't move. He was staring at me. Then he remembered where he knew me from. His reaction wasn't what I expected. His eyes jumped, and he stepped back into the apartment with his left hand clutching into a fist. Not a belligerent fist, a nervous fist.

"You're that L.A. detective out at the warehouse. Mr. Boetter said we don't talk to you. Shaw, yeh."

"I'm not here to talk about Boetter. I'm here to talk about Lillian Marsak and you."

He didn't try to stop me coming into the apartment. His muscles were all for good looks, narcissistic. His smooth round face was chalky, the dark little mustache standing out as if painted on. He was nervous, and more—scared. The loud music blared. I didn't think he was aware of it. I was. I never did like *My Fair Lady*. Maybe because I played in *Pygmalion* myself. I turned off the machine. Sobers didn't protest.

"Sit down," I said. When you have a man scared, push.

He sat down on a cheap, gaudy modern armchair. The whole big room was gaudy, from the red couch to the free-form glass coffee table to the poles of directional lights with blue and red bulbs. I looked into the bedroom. The king-sized bed was red enamel, the shag rug was black and so thick I could have sunk to the ankles, and there were four mirrors. The dining room had candles on a teak table. The bedroom closet was full of sharp clothes. A truckdriver who saw himself as a dapper swinger off the job. A jealous self-image?

"How long did you go with Lillian Marsak?" I said.

"Maybe six months, that's all."

"That's long enough. How long did you know she was going to dump you?"

"Couple of weeks before she got . . . killed."

"She told you?"

"I guessed." Sobers said, lit a cigarette with shaky hands. "You can tell. I been around. They get snotty, hard to handle. You know, kind of they don't care what you think any more."

I watched the cigarette tremble in his mouth. "You're scared as a nervous rabbit. Why?"

"Your broad gets bombed, you'd be nervous," Sobers said. He seemed to hunch in the red chair. "I been scared ever since it happened. I mean, she was my girl, she was playing with some new guy. Any day the sheriff could get ideas."

"But the bomb was for Russell Dobson."

"That maybe don't stop them coming to me. They don't find anyone bombed Dobson, they'll be after me."

"That's all?"

"I don't like cops. They scare me."

"Maybe you knew all along it wasn't Dobson the killer went after, it was Lillian Marsak."

"No way. Only it makes me nervous. She was—"

"Every way, Sobers," I said. "It wasn't Dobson in the target, it was Lillian. I know that now. You must have been pretty mad when you guessed she was dumping you."

"Mad?" He shook his head violently. "Sure I was mad, but not enough to—to—murder the dame!"

"Where were you that Monday?"

"Nowhere. I took the day off. I . . . I went fishing, yeh. Alone. No one saw me."

"Fishing?" I looked around that gaudy seduction pit. It wasn't the apartment of a man who fished. "What kind of fish?"

He sweated. "Bass."

"No," I said.

He wilted. "All right. You know what I did that day? I tried to get a date with Lillian! How about that? All day I called her at her store. No luck. She was busy. Damn her!"

He glared up at me. Then, suddenly, his face seemed to almost melt like wax. "It was her they wanted dead? I mean, how do you know? Lillian?"

"I have ways, and I'm sure. So you've got no alibi at all?"

"She wouldn't see me. So I got drunk. Right here, four P.M. on. Real, stinking drunk. I didn't hear till next day."

He sat like a man who remembered the taste of every glass he had drunk that night. A bitter taste. As if somehow he had failed his woman and himself, his fine body, by getting drunk all alone while she was being killed. Or a man sorry for himself over being mixed up in it at all. If it wasn't all a lie.

"Who was her new man, Sobers?"

"She never said, nossir. Some big shot around here, though. She said she nearly had it made at last. A big time ahead. A future. She said I'd be a two-bit truckdriver with big ideas all my life."

"That made you even madder, didn't it?"

"Sure it did. To hell with her."

"What were you in the Army, Sobers?"

He was at least forty-five, and that was World War II when everyone was in the service.

"Armor," he said, "but I don't know nothing about bombs."

"Anyone can learn from an army manual."

He stubbed out his cigarette, lit another. "Why would I kill her? I do good with women. What's one? You think I'm the kind who kills 'cause she leaves him? Love? Anyway, it'd be the guy I'd kill, wouldn't it?"

"No, not if you got to hate Lillian."

"Look, I'm scared just thinking maybe the cops'll come and talk to me. I got no guts, none," he confessed. "She was right about me, you know? I got no guts, and I'm no good at anything except driving a truck and talking to women. I'm real good with women, believe me. In bed. I'm not much out of bed. The sack is all I am good at. Nowhere to go. Lil was right."

Somehow, I believed him. He did do well with women, he was good in bed. There were plenty who would envy him. But he wouldn't keep a woman long, no, unless she needed a stud very much more than most women did.

"She gave you nothing about her new man?"

"She used to meet him somewhere. Not in the open, you know? Maybe he's married."

"Did you take her address book?"

"What the hell for? It's all men."

"You remember any of the names in it?"

"No."

He sweated. He could be lying—about everything, or about part of it. His left fist still clenched like a vise. He put out his cigarette again.

"Look," he said, "you want to know about her new guy, go ask a girl named Ginny Piper."

"You think she knows who the man is?"

"Sure," Walt Sobers said. "Lil told me she had to

thank Ginny for meeting the guy. She laughed like hell about it, said Ginny sure missed out on a good thing.''

As I went out he lit another cigarette, sat staring at his gaudy apartment with all its cheap finery as if seeing what was beyond it and not liking what he saw. His future.

27

GINNY PIPER WAS glad to go to lunch. I picked her up at the Markham Arms, took her to the restaurant at the Redwood Inn. She was overdressed in a green cocktail dress, but that usually had a way of intriguing tired businessmen.

"What do you do for a living, Ginny?" I asked when we'd settled in a corner booth with drinks in hand.

"Public stenographer," she said, drank a lot of her martini. "That's where I work, an office downtown."

She meant, even if she didn't say so, that where she worked wasn't necessarily where she made her living. Even in Fort Smith, or maybe especially in the Fort Smiths of the country, a pretty young woman who wanted "more" had other ways of making a good living than badly paid work.

"You take a lot of time off?"

"I work when I want. We've got a pool of girls. We get sent all over to take notes, type, you know."

"What were you doing the Monday Lillian Marsak was killed? I mean, before you were in The Pines bar with her?"

"Most Mondays I take off. Sunday can be rough."

"How old are you, Ginny?"

She put down her martini slowly. "Twenty-six, why?"

It wasn't the question a man asked a girl the first time he took her out—even if this date was business. She was wary.

"Ever been in the Army? Around soldiers?"

"No." Her eyes grew large. "You want to know if I can make a bomb! That's it, isn't it? Me? You are crazy!"

"You were in The Pines with her when Dobson picked her up. You knew she would take him to her car. Maybe when you went to make those telephone calls—"

"Why would I want to murder Lillian?!"

"Maybe because you introduced her to her new man, her big catch. Maybe she took him away from you. You don't plan to be a public stenographer all your life, do you?"

"Introduced her? Who told you that? I don't even know who the man is."

She was talking loudly, angry. People in the restaurant were watching us. I noticed a woman far down at the end of the bar near the door who seemed familiar, but I couldn't see her face. Turned away from me, yet I had the impression she had been looking at us a moment before I looked at her.

"It won't work, Ginny," I said. "Lillian told someone that she had you to thank for meeting the new man. She was amused, said you'd missed out on a good thing."

"I never introduced her to a man! You think I'm crazy? Lillian? I'd as soon have introduced any man I knew to Mata Hari. I had the looks and the age, but Lillian had a way, believe me. Who told you Lillian said that?"

"Walt Sobers."

She shook her head. "Why would he do that? He's got nothing against me."

"You're sure you don't know who the man is?"

"Why would I lie? Lillian was my friend."

"I can think of reasons."

"You mean to protect him? Well, you're wrong. I've got two steadies, a couple of occasionals, and none of them knew Lillian even to say hello."

I thought for a while. The woman who seemed familiar was still at the bar, but hidden by a group of businessmen drinking their lunch. Why would Walt Sobers lie about Ginny Piper?

"Let's say Sobers is telling the truth," I said. "Lillian said what she said: she had you to thank for meeting this man. If she didn't mean an introduction, what could she have meant? Did you tell her about men you met?"

"Tell her?" Ginny Piper frowned into her martini. "Well, yes, sometimes. We'd sometimes tell each other about interesting men we'd run into. On the job, at a party, you know."

"What men did you meet in the last months you might have told her about?"

"God, there's so many," she said, finished her martini. "I mean, I go and do stenographic work for a lot of companies and businessmen in town. There could have been twenty. Anyone."

"Do you remember their names, just any names?"

She shook her head. "No, not offhand. We keep a record at the office, though. I mean, who we work for. But what good would it do you? Maybe twenty names, maybe more? Sometimes we just enter the company name."

"But Lillian could have meant that? You'd met, maybe done work for, some man and he sounded good to her. She managed to meet him, and was one up on you?"

"She could have, I guess, yes."

"Only, you can't think of anyone it could be? She gave you no hint at all?"

"No, none."

"And she wasn't worried about anything?"

"Not that she told me," she said, then suddenly frowned. "Well, except—" She looked at her martini glass as if she wished it weren't empty. I waited. She looked up. "Maybe a week before she got . . . killed, she went to visit her folks. She didn't get along with her father. The only time she went out there was when she was feeling low, or maybe worried. I mean, that's how it usually was. She didn't seem low this time."

"Unless she was too scared of something to show it."

Ginny Piper shivered. "Poor Lillian. All she wanted was something good out of life."

"That's sometimes too much to want," I said.

I ordered another martini for her and some lunch. While we ate she asked me about my work. When she heard I was married to Maureen Shaw it seemed to excite her. I could see the dream in her eyes—to be Maureen Shaw, famous and admired and rich. To be the result, without any understanding of the hard work, of what Maureen Shaw really was, of how unimportant the fame and glamor were to a real Maureen Shaw.

"God, it must be great to be so famous, have everything."

"No, it's not great. Sometimes it's great to know you do very good work, but not often. There's always better to be done."

She would never understand that. You have to live with the curse of the obligation to do something to understand it, to know that the by-product of fame is irrelevant. So I asked her about her life in Fort Smith. A dull life, but simple, and in its way with more pleasure than Maureen's life. She wouldn't understand that, either.

While we waited for our coffee, she went to the rest room. I watched her go, a pretty woman. I sensed rather than saw the shadow standing over our table.

"You don't waste time. Anything in a skirt."

Nancy Cathcart looked down at me, her face pinched. She wore the youngest dress I'd seen her in—short, slim, tight to her breasts. Each dress freer, and yet her face pinched. Could I be angry? The battle inside her.

"She was Lillian Marsak's friend," I said. "Just work."

"I thought I was work. But why not some fun, too, yes?"

"I don't apologize for last night."

She sat down. "I do. I'm sorry about last night."

"For me, or for yourself?"

"For both of us." Her eyes were large, a depth in them. "I could feel the nightgown against my breasts. Heavy. I felt I wanted you to lift the nightgown. I wanted your eyes on me. I've thought about a psychiatrist. A Cathcart doesn't do that, though."

"How long have you been like that?"

"All my life. Cathcart walls," she said. She toyed with an empty cup. "There was a time, once, when I thought it could be different. I had a sister, Peggy. Two years older. There was a man who wanted to marry her, she said. She went off with someone else instead. He used her. She died."

"And you closed up all the way."

"We were the last Cathcarts. She tried to be different, to be a woman, and it left me alone. If I try, will I vanish, have no one? No more Cathcarts?"

"Maybe you'd find the last Cathcart."

"With a casual married man passing through? With

some man who thinks of nothing but himself? You and Campbell Grant. Is that the kind of man a frozen woman always finds? Or a Dobson? The morally dead, the egomaniacs and the transients?"

I had no answer. Yes, that was the probable answer. A woman who begins from a psychological wound will find the imperfect, will seek it, frightened by the whole man. But could I say that, and before I could think of something else to say, Ginny Piper came back. The younger girl looked at Nancy Cathcart.

"Double date, Mr. Shaw?" she said.

Nancy Cathcart stood up as if slapped. "I'm sorry, Miss—?"

"Piper," I said. "Virginia Piper, Nancy Cathcart. Nancy is working with me, Ginny. Is there anything else you can tell me about Lillian?"

"Nothing I can think of. You can take me home."

"Finish your coffee, and give me her parents' address."

Ginny Piper sat down. So did Nancy Cathcart. The address was number 4, Hill Road, Willis Corners.

"I know where it is," Nancy Cathcart said. "Can I go with you, Paul? Today?"

"If you want to," I said.

Ginny Piper finished her one cup of coffee. She didn't want a second. Another woman annoyed her. I took her back to the Markham Arms. Nancy Cathcart rode in silence with us.

"Thanks for the lunch," Ginny Piper said.

Her voice said she had expected more than a lunch. She walked away with a stiff back.

28

ON ANY MAP of California, between the main highway into Fort Smith—U.S. 101—and Interstate Highway 5, there is the empty white space of the Coast Range. Willis Corners is in that white space. A hamlet from the past: general store, gas station, a few frame houses set on steep hills, and a narrow blacktop back road that leads off the almost-as-narrow marked county highway.

The late-afternoon sun slanted down through the tall pines into the steep canyons of heavy forest and sparse clearings as Nancy Cathcart and I drove slowly along the narrow blacktop looking for Hill Road. The country reminded me of the mountains of Vermont, except for one thing—size. Here the mountains were higher, the boulders bigger, the canyons deeper, the slopes steeper, the trees taller, the creeks wider. In Vermont a man walked the trails, here he rode. He rode if he hoped to survive to return. Only the houses and farms were much the same. The land bigger, but not man.

We found Hill Road cutting sharply off the blacktop, and number 4 about a half a mile in. A two-story frame house that had been white but needed paint. Steep fields rose on both sides. The yard was littered with rusting farm equipment and two old cars falling slowly to pieces. A battered pickup truck and an equally battered Ford sat in a dirt driveway. An unpainted barn leaned behind the house, and there was no garage.

A heavy woman with a pale, yellowing face came out onto the small porch of the house as Nancy and I walked up toward the front door from the driveway below. She was about fifty-five but looked older, and wore a faded print dress that could have done little to keep out the chill of the almost sunless canyon. Her fat wasn't the fat of too much, but of too little. An unhealthy fat that came from a starch diet and indolence.

"You want something?" she said in a harsh voice.

"Mrs. Marsak?" I asked.

"What do you want?"

"I want to talk about Lillian," I said.

"She's dead. What is there to talk about?" The harsh voice of the fat old woman broke a little, softened.

"Her death, Mrs. Marsak. Her murder."

From inside the house behind the old woman, a thin, sharp voice reached us. A belligerent voice.

"Bring him in here. You got work."

Mrs. Marsak turned without a word and went into the house. She left the door open. We went in after her. There was a narrow hall with doors off it. Through the open doorways I saw a neglected dining room, dust on the chairs; a stiff room of hard-looking upholstered furniture that would once have been called the parlor; a rear kitchen with a potbellied stove and an old table with the remains of a meal on it; and an untidy sitting room with a television set and rumpled throws on the chairs and couch. All the rooms were small, closed in. The winters were hard in these mountains, and fuel cost money.

"In here," the thin male voice said.

We went into the untidy sitting room. A tall, angular man in faded overalls half lay on the rug-covered couch. He wore heavy boots and a wide-brimmed hat and was smoking a cigarette. His eyes were small and angry—a perpetual anger—around a bony nose and a thin mouth.

"Who are you?" the man said.

"Paul Shaw. A private detective working on your daughter's murder, Mr. Marsak."

"What for?"

"You don't want her murderer caught?"

"She had it coming. Never listened to me. A slut. Ran out on me, and me a sick man. No son, no, and no son-in-law to help me. I fed her, she owed me."

"Didn't you owe her something?" Nancy Cathcart said.

The tall, belligerent man looked at Nancy. "Who's she? One of my slut's city friends? Another whore?"

"She's my friend," I said. "What do you farm here, Marsak?"

"Trouble and a busted back. You go back to the city, find her murderer if you want. It don't matter none to me."

I had sensed the old woman hovering somewhere behind me since we came in. Not in the littered sitting room, out in the hall. Listening, but not wanting to be seen. Now she came in. A few steps into the room, nervous. "They told us it was some accident," she said. "Lillian got killed because she was with some politician they wanted to kill."

"No," I said. "They were wrong. It was the politician who was killed by accident. The murderer wanted Lillian dead. I came to ask if you knew why, or even who?"

The tall man said, "I heard all about it, mister. That whole State Park fight. They take good land away from poor men and give it to the government, let it rot. So kids and schoolteachers can look at it. They give it away to the goddamn lumbermen, the city crooks rob an honest man. I got no use for politicians, or parks, or them big lumbermen. None of them. Give me them trees, I cut down every one of them.''

"No," I said. "It was Lillian the killer wanted to kill.''

"Why?" the old woman said.

"That's what I hoped to find out here. She came out to see you a few weeks ago. What did she talk about? Did she name anyone she was worried about? Was she scared of—''

"Scared of hellfire," the man said, spat into a bucket on the floor. "Scared of what she was. A whore. Wouldn't marry a decent man, bring him home here to help me. Left me and her mother to break our backs on the rocks and snow.''

The old woman said, "Why should she have stayed here? To break her back, too? She made a better life than I ever had. A woman has power in what God gave her. Why not use what her body gave her to use? If that's a way to some life.''

"Talk, old woman. You ruined her, ruined me giving her those whore ideas. Go and do your work, damn you.''

I said, "She came out here, Lillian. What did she say? Why did she come? Did she talk about any man, or men? Did—''

Lillian's father sat up. "Go back to the city. Go on! We don't know nothing. Her men? You don't come out here and talk about her men. She's dead, good riddance.''

"Mr. Marsak, I—''

He pointed to a corner of the room. A shotgun leaned there. "I can use that. Trespassing. Go on.''

We left the littered sitting room.

29

ON THE NARROW porch there was almost no light left. Late afternoon, but at the bottom of the wooded canyon there was little sun. Already growing cold in the blue shadows as Nancy Cathcart and I walked down the steep slope to my car.

"Mr. Shaw?"

The old woman stood there in the gloom.

"I'm sorry," she said. "He is a bad man, but where else can I go?"

"That's up to you, Mrs. Marsak."

"Paul!" Nancy Cathcart said.

"No, he's right," Mrs. Marsak said. "Only I can help myself, and I won't. It takes courage to leave the familiar, no matter how bad, for the unknown. You invent a way of getting through each day, build a rut that is at least tolerable. I need him, he needs me. But Lillian escaped, yes. I am proud of that. Her escape was the one thing I did. Now—" She stepped closer to me, fat and old. "You say this murderer wanted to kill Lillian, after all? Not that Dobson?"

"Yes," I said. "Why?"

"Because she was angry when she came here the last time. Angry and nervous, a little. Lillian was a strong woman, she didn't get nervous easily. She laughed about it this time, but under her laugh she was uneasy, I know that."

"Laughed about what? Why angry?"

"Some trouble with one of her past men. An unimportant man, one she had been with not very much. She was annoyed by him. She called him 'an ape.' I think he called here that weekend looking for her. It made her very angry."

"Do you know his name?"

"No. She never told me any names because she was afraid Mr. Marsak would make me tell him, and then go into Fort Smith and try to make trouble for them, get money."

"You know nothing at all about this man?"

"His voice. An odd voice. Very nervous, heavy, almost a sick voice. Lillian wouldn't talk about him. She said she would settle it once and for all."

"But he was an *old* friend?"

"Yes."

"What do you know about a new friend?"

The old woman looked up toward the summit of the steep canyon rim as if the sunlight up there was at the edge of the world. The end of her world, beyond which were only dreams or monsters. Her voice was low, no longer harsh, talking about the hopes of her daughter, who would have no more hopes.

"She was excited," she said. "He wasn't rich, but he was going to be, she was sure. He was going to be important. It was her break, she said. What she'd been waiting for. That made it even more important to settle finally with the one who was bothering her. She wasn't going to let past mistakes ruin her this time, she said. This was her chance.''

Nancy Cathcart walked away, around the car, and got into her seat. She looked straight ahead through the windshield at the long, dark canyon shadows. The old woman brushed once at her eyes. She probably hadn't cried in a lot of years, her life too bad to cry about. Her daughter's one big chance had come, but sudden death had taken that chance away before it could become reality.

"But you don't know his name? This new man?"

"No."

"Could this big chance have involved anything dangerous?"

"Dangerous?"

"Something she knew? Blackmail? A squeeze on the man?"

The old woman looked all around at the crumbling farm. "I don't know, but what wouldn't you do for a chance if you came from here?"

I made my voice gentle. "Was this man married, maybe?"

"I don't think so. They were keeping it quiet, but I think for some other reason. They met at some beach house in Fort Smith. She didn't tell me that, but she talked a lot about this beach house, and I knew it was where they met. A beautiful house, she said, at the very end of some lane on the water. Jacon Lane, yes, that was it. A funny name. All fine houses on that lane, she said, and this one was the best because it was the last.''

Police work is a frustrating business. You know the answers are there, but you don't know where to ask the questions. When you do know where to ask, the answers can come almost too easily. I thanked the old woman and got into my car beside Nancy Cathcart.

As we drove back down Hill Road I saw the old woman still standing in the cold canyon shadows. She was in no hurry to go into her house.

30

JACON LANE WAS a short street down to the ocean in the most exclusive shore section of Fort Smith. It was night when we turned into the lane, the sound of the October surf heavy on the beach ahead, and the beach houses of the rich were mostly dark. Set back behind lawns and trees, they were deserted now by their owners who had retreated with the coming of winter to their bigger and warmer houses inland.

The last house was smaller than most, had no lawn but was built into the natural rock above the narrow northern beach, and faced out to sea. Built of dark native redwood, its walls were glass, and a redwood deck surrounded three sides. A sign offered it for sale, but it didn't look empty, and there were fresh tire marks in the gravel drive up to a garage open under the house itself.

I parked at the end of the lane in a turnaround wet from the night spray of the surf, and we walked back through the cold, wet wind. Light showed bright through the front glass wall that faced the ocean. The entrance was up stairs at the rear from the gravel drive. No one answered my ring. I left Nancy at the rear, circled around on the high deck to the uncurtained front wall.

Through the glass I saw what had so impressed Lillian Marsak. The room inside, lighted by two tall, slim redwood lamps, was warm and rich. Expensive and with taste; modern and yet natural. The furniture and materials were the sleek work of the best craftsmen, and yet it all seemed to fit with the reflection of the wild ocean and the rocks and trees all around the house. The big living room seemed to occupy the whole house, with a kitchen at the rear. A balcony cantilevered out over the main room was where the bedrooms must be.

I tried the sliding glass doors. They were open. I went in and through the living room to the rear entrance. Nancy Cathcart came in shivering from the night wind and damp. She stood in the beautiful living room of the fine house and looked around. A large abstract painting on the one solid wall caught her eye.

"I know this house, yes," she said, stared at the painting. "I was here once, years ago. It belongs to one of the big lumbermen. Catlett, yes. Marshall Catlett. He has a mansion out at the edge of the State Park."

"Lillian Marsak had really hit the jackpot."

"No," Nancy shook her head. "Marshall Catlett is an old man, over seventy. I'd heard he was leaving Fort Smith, buying a place in the Bahamas for his health."

"The place is up for sale," I said. "Who would he rent to? Or lend it?"

Her voice took on that stiff, bitter edge. "For a love nest? That is the phrase, isn't it? A place to cheat your wife with some woman, and then cheat the woman later."

"One of his fellow lumbermen?" I said.

Before I could suggest anything else, or name any names, I heard a car turn into Jacon Lane and come fast. I listened. The car turned into the driveway of the beach house and stopped. Heavy footsteps crunched in the gravel. I motioned Nancy into the far corner away from the door, got behind the door with my revolver. The steps did not hesitate coming up the stairs to the door, he had not noticed my car parked at the end of the lane. He used a key on the door and strode into the house, turning directly toward the kitchen, a bag in his hands. He stopped.

He had swung the door closed behind him without looking back. Not consciously looking back. But by reflex his eyes had glanced behind to see the door swing shut, and after three more steps he stopped. He had seen me when the door closed. Stopped with his back to me. Rigid. I didn't have to see his face.

"Nice place you've got here, Grant," I said.

Campbell Grant turned. The brown paper bag still held in both hands. A bag of potato chips stuck out at the top of the bag, the rectangular shape of the bottom of the bag looked like a six-pack. The feast of a solitary man at the TV set. The tall blond campaign manager's blue eyes had a strange shine, almost a feeling of relief in them as he looked at me.

"So you found me," he said, relief in his voice, too. "I wondered if you really would. I could have stayed away from here, but that wouldn't have mattered. You'd have found my name on the rental."

"One of your lumberman pals rented it to you so you could have an impressive place to dazzle Lillian Marsak?"

"One of my lumberman pals did that, yes. To hide, too. In Fort Smith, Lillian didn't have a very good reputation, and I'm just getting a solid start. A year, maybe, and I'd be established, and then when I married her that would have been okay."

"Marry?"

"Shocked, Shaw?"

"No," I said. "Surprised. You don't strike me as the marrying kind any more than Dobson was."

Nancy Cathcart stepped out from her corner where Campbell Grant hadn't seen her. "You planned to marry her? Or was that just the normal male game of lies?"

"You, too, Nancy?" Grant said. "Well we've got quite a quorum, haven't we. Just let me put this stuff in the kitchen. Can I offer anyone a beer? Afraid it's all I have."

Neither Nancy nor I answered him. He shrugged, went into the kitchen area with his bag. He took out the potato chips and two six-packs of beer. He opened one can, put the others in the refrigerator, came back out, sat down on a fine chrome and soft-leather chair, crossed his long legs.

"I was a captain in the Army," Grant said. "Ordnance, too. I know all about bombs."

"How long were you together, Grant?"

"About a month before. Not long, but enough. She was quite a woman. We saw the same world. A pair of whores against the rest of the world. I've always seen this world as an enemy, a place I had to beat, a sheep pasture. Lil and I were a pair of wolves among the sheep.

"Funny. Here I was up in this backwater looking for a chance to take over. Alone, out of my element, looking for any woman to take care of my nerves. Even Nancy there. The ice queen." He smiled.

She went pale, but she said nothing. I didn't look at her. Campbell Grant went on smiling.

"I'd have taken any woman I could get to say yes," he said, "and then I find a woman just perfect for me. *The* woman. Something a man almost never finds under the best conditions, and I found her when I was frustrated enough to take anything."

"You thought she felt the same?" I said.

"I knew she felt the same."

"You were sure, but she didn't, did she? She wanted you, her big chance, but she couldn't stop going with any man who beckoned to her."

"No, she had stopped. She wanted me."

"When she let Dobson pick her up like any common B-girl, you killed her."

"No. She wouldn't have let him pick her up."

"She did, Grant."

"Yes. I can't think of an explanation yet. There is one."

"She went with Dobson that evening, so you killed her."

"She loved me. I was her big chance. Our chance," Campbell Grant said, drank his beer. "But if it had happened that way, how could I have been ready with the bomb? She hadn't been near Russ Dobson before that night."

"There were others," I said. "Not just Dobson. You hated her, planned it, Dobson was just a coincidence."

"No. I loved her. I trusted her. I wasn't even there."

Nancy went into the kitchen area and opened a can of beer. She seemed to be looking somewhere beyond the room where Campbell Grant insisted on his love, *their* love. I sat down, lit a cigarette.

"If you didn't kill her," I said, "how did you know she was the real victim? You've known that all along, haven't you? The only one who did. That's why you fired me, wanted the investigation to stop. You knew it had to lead to you. You knew Lillian was the real victim, and yet you hired us. Why?"

"Yes, I knew," Grant said, drank. "I'm not a fool. I know politics. I had a year plus to learn about politics here. No one would have gained by killing Dobson. You know now that Sam MacGruder had Dobson back in his pocket, and Tom Allen could only lose by violence. Jesse Boetter might have wanted Dobson dead for his personal ambition, or I might have hoped to take Dobson's place. But I didn't see Boetter killing for ambition, and I knew I hadn't. I couldn't think of anyone who really wanted Russ Dobson dead.

"So it had to be Lillian. It was her car, after all. Someone had killed her, I had no idea who or why. But if anyone else realized that, my relationship with her would have to come out. I'd be a prime suspect. I'd be in trouble here, and just when Dobson's death gave me an opening. I would have risked a lot for Lillian, but she was dead. Why risk now?

"I decided to hire a detective from far outside to try to make sure the political motive was kept going. I thought I could make sure an outside detective was convinced that Dobson was the victim, Lillian an accident. It was a mistake. I knew it almost as soon as I got back here from L.A. An unnecessary risk, the sheriff had no ideas beyond Dobson as the victim. I had made a mistake, gotten confused in a panic.

"Then Sam MacGruder approached me about maybe running for the state senate if the poll-boycott rumors and a possible recall proved true. If Jesse Boetter got too many citizens against him, MacGruder would back me as a Dobson man. So I'd made a double mistake, risked keeping the investigation going, stirring up trouble, when MacGruder wanted it all calmed."

"MacGruder takes no chances," I said.

"I realized my mistake, tried to fire you. I didn't know then about Delaney, the attack on you. You wouldn't let me fire you. Since then I've been waiting. Maybe you wouldn't realize it had been Lillian the bomber wanted.

Maybe you'd fail, give up and leave, and no one would know about Lil and me.''

"That's all you were worried about? Your reputation? No, it's not good enough.''

He shook his head. "I wouldn't kill Lillian, never. I knew her past, about her men. If I'd had a reason to murder anyone it would have been Dobson. He was in my way. But he wasn't the target, was he?''

"She had a date to meet someone about six P.M., Grant. Who else except you?''

"I don't know who else,'' Grant said. "It wasn't me. I had been busy with Dobson's work all day, planned to meet Lil later that night after the banquet Dobson was to speak at. When Dobson canceled our conference for MacGruder, I came back here to work alone. I worked out on the deck, some neighbors saw me. Down for the day they were.''

"They saw you all the time?''

"No, not all the time. I went inside at times. But my car never left.''

"You could walk up the beach, have another car ready at the next street.''

"I didn't.''

"Then who was she meeting at six o'clock? And where?''

"She didn't tell me who or where. Someone from her past who was bothering her again, and we'd agreed never to discuss the past. Burying a mistake, she said, something she had to finish. Short and sweet, she told me, she could meet me by six-thirty if I wanted. I had the banquet to attend, so we made it for later. That's all I know.''

"A man bothering her? Walt Sobers?''

"We never mentioned names. I told you that.''

"Yes, you told me,'' I said. "All this time you knew she was the prime victim, knew she had a date to meet

someone at the time she was killed, and you said nothing.
You were in love, but you made no move to help find her
killer.''

"She was dead,'' Campbell Grant said. "Why risk
trouble for myself? What does it matter who killed her?''

Nancy Cathcart put down her beer can, came out of the
kitchen area. "The woman is dead, what does it matter? A
dead woman is no use to any man, is she? She can't give
you what you want, so forget her. Did you ever think,
Campbell, that she might have been killed *because* of you?
Because she let you love her, she's dead? Destroyed!''

"I've thought about it,'' Campbell Grant said.

He stood, went to get another can of beer.

31

"DO YOU BELIEVE him, Paul?" Nancy Cathcart said.

We sat in my car above the angry sea again. A wind rising hard and fast, blowing the invisible night ocean into sharp glows of white all across our view.

"How the hell can I know yet?" I was feeling angry. Campbell Grant could have saved two days' work, and there was no way of knowing how much more he could tell, guilty or innocent. Who else was holding back, if not outright lying?

"What will you do now?" Nancy Cathcart asked.

"I don't know. But I'll take you home first."

It was a lie, I knew what I was going to do next. I wanted to work alone. I was tired of her cold hang-up—the evil of men. A fetish she couldn't forget for a moment, always there on the tip of her tongue. How unfair the world was to women, unfair for making women at all—for making men need them and not as pals! I didn't fool her, no.

"All right," she said. "I am sorry about last night,

Paul. I can't help it. Not since Peggy died. I've learned to understand, in my head, blame no one. But my body won't understand.''

"Your body understands," I said. "It's your brain."

"Yes, I suppose so."

I said, "I'll call you later. You'll be home?"

"I . . . I can't promise I'll—"

"I didn't ask you to."

I started the car, backed viciously and drove out of Jacon Lane. I was angry for more than one reason. A simple case was being made complicated by side issues, the twists and turns of Fort Smith life. Someone had wanted Lillian Marsak dead, and had made a date to meet her at six that night. It was that simple—but someone was complicating it with politics, lies and hired gunmen. Why? Or maybe I was complicating it just by being in it, nosing into where I threatened people I didn't even know about.

"I'll be here, Paul," Nancy said when I dropped her in front of her house.

"Sure," I said.

I drove straight to Walt Sobers' apartment. The garish Buick was in the driveway, dim light on up in Sobers' apartment. Blue light. Maybe the truckdriver ex-lover of Lillian Marsak wasn't alone. I didn't give a damn if he was alone or not. I went up and knocked hard.

I could feel the silence inside. A record playing very low this time, and yet silent. A suspended silence.

"Sobers!"

I heard movement. The truckdriver's voice. "Who is it?"

"Paul Shaw! Open up."

Walt Sobers stood in the doorway with the blue light

behind him. "You son-of-a-bitch! You sicked the cops on me!"

Both fists clenched this time, and those muscles bulged under another of his Ban-Lon shirts. But I knew him now, he was all cardboard. I pushed him back into the room. It wasn't very bold, I was twice his size and fifteen years younger even if he had any notion of using those muscles.

"I didn't sick anyone on you. They were here?"

"Half the damn day! Quigley's been questioning me for hours. I'm so groggy I don't know my own name. If you didn't send them, who did? They knew it was Lillian."

"Quigley could have figured it out, he's no fool. Or maybe someone I talked to told him. What did he want to know?"

"Same as you. Who hated her. Where was I. Who were her other men. They never stopped hammering."

In that blue-lit room with its low, soft music he was scared. His fists shook, and his eyes were like the eyes of a stray dog panting in terror. There was no one else in the cheap room. Sobers had been sitting alone in the seductive blue light listening to soft music and shaking.

"They'll hammer more if I tell them what I know now," I said. "I've found her new man, the big shot. He's got an alibi, but Lillian told him she was going to finish off a past mistake. That was her six P.M. appointment—with some man who was chasing and bothering her. You admitted you'd been phoning her all that day trying to get her to see you."

"But she wouldn't!" He sat down on rubber legs. "I told you. She wouldn't, so I got drunk."

"Maybe." I bent down close to his face in the eerie blue light. I felt like something out of a surrealist movie, the evil Dr. Caligari. "And maybe you badgered her until she said she'd meet you at six that day. Maybe you badgered her until she had to tell you to your face you were history. And maybe that's how you planned it—so you could set your bomb!''

His face could have been dead for a month in that blue light, the small mustache the final touch of a master embalmer. All around us that low, sweet show music seemed to fill every corner. A trick he'd probably worked on for days to create just the right effect for seducing some romantic little shop girl who thought he was sophisticated.

"No," he whispered, almost gagged.

"Yes. Who else? You'd been her steady for six months. Who else was badgering her?"

He was almost in shock, like a robot. "I tried to get her to meet me. She wouldn't. I called her at the shop all day. She wouldn't talk to me. She wouldn't go out. She was busy. Busy . . . busy . . ."

I'd seen men groggy from punches—punch-drunk. I'd seen men in shock from fatigue in Vietnam. I'd seen them babble, talk like mindless robots, from being strung out too long with tension. Walt Sobers was groggy from fear, in shock from too many words. Punch-drunk on words. Every word I said was like hitting him over and over.

"Busy with what? Busy fighting you off?"

"She wouldn't go out. She wouldn't even see me. She said I shouldn't try to see her any more. She said I shouldn't play any smart tricks like going to The Pines to meet her at the bar. She said she'd make Jack Ready or Ben Wheeler throw me out. She said she had important business at The Pines at six o'clock. She said if I tried to butt in she'd—"

"Business? At six o'clock that night? At The Pines?"

"She said if I went there I was finished for—"

"The Pines, Sobers? You're sure her six P.M. business was *at* The Pines?"

"Finished, she said. You know, I was glad. Yeh, glad. She said—"

He was still sitting there in the blue light talking to his low music when I closed the door behind me.

He was good in bed with women, and at nothing else, and I didn't think he'd be quite the same again.

32

Jack Ready, the terrier man in the sharp race-track clothes, was at the guard table in The Pines as I headed back for Salvatore Vasto's office. The after-dinner time at the roadhouse was busy, well-dressed men and women at every table, packed into the bar. The city might look like Iowa, but its nightlife was more like New York and Los Angeles. Then, even Iowa nightlife was like New York and Los Angeles these days.

"Is he in?" I asked Ready.

"Yeh. Go on back, he said you're okay."

Salvatore Vasto was eating a late dinner at his desk as I went in. The door in the side wall was open, a bottle of wine stood on the desk beside his steak. Château Ausone, 1953. Vasto knew his wine and treated himself well—his private cellar. I sat down. He poured a glass, offered me one. I took it. Food or no, I didn't refuse a '53 Ausone.

"You look like you've come up with something," Vasto said, sipped his wine, half closed his heavy eyes.

"We found out Dobson and Lillian didn't have a date,"

I said. "You wondered how anyone could have figured Dobson would be in her car."

"I remember," he said, sipped. "It wasn't Dobson the killer was after, right? It was Lillian."

"How long have you known?"

"I don't know, but I guessed. After you left. I got to thinking, right? I thought—it was her, and . . ."

"And what?"

"Nothing. Go ahead, what have you come up with?"

He covered himself, but I couldn't miss it. He had more on his mind than just a realization that Lillian Marsak had been the target. He knew something I didn't yet.

"She had no date with Dobson, but she did have a date. No, not a date, a meeting. A brief meeting to kiss off some man from her past who was bothering her too much. Short and sweet, nothing that would interfere with an evening with Dobson. A meeting right here. At your place."

Vasto shook his head. "I trust my bartender. Lillian Marsak met no one here except Dobson."

"Not inside your place, Vasto—in your parking lot."

"In my lot?"

"In her car. The man set it up that way so he would be sure she would be in her car—*here*. He put the bomb in her car when she drove in at her usual time, had made the date to meet her at her car so she'd be sure to go to it soon after he put in the bomb. For some reason, Vasto, the killer wanted her to be *here*."

"Why would he want that?" Vasto said, looked away.

"Maybe because he was afraid he'd be noticed if he tried to plant the bomb anywhere else, but here he wouldn't be."

Vasto said nothing, sipped at his wine again. But he wasn't really tasting it now, great as it was.

"Or because anywhere else he'd have had to alibi his

time, and that scared him, but here he wouldn't need an alibi. Here was a natural place for him to meet Lillian Marsak, she thought nothing about him asking to meet her in your parking lot. It was logical, normal. All he had to do was set it up, plant the bomb he had ready, not show at six o'clock, and she'd get mad and drive off.''

"Why was it logical to meet here? An alibi here?''

"Because he belonged here, Vasto. This was where he was supposed to be between five and six that evening.''

The roadhouse owner was silent for over a minute. He held his wine glass, but he didn't drink. I drank, and waited. It was marvelous wine, but my mind wasn't on it. Vasto sighed.

"Yeh,'' he said. "I thought about him, but I didn't want to, right? Like finding out some big, dumb dog is sick, bit someone. You feel lousy. You know it isn't really his fault. You know he got fooled, goaded, hurt bad, and something snapped inside and he bit. Just a big, slow animal couldn't think straight. Sad.''

"Ben Wheeler?'' I said.

Vasto nodded. "I heard rumors, maybe a year ago, eight months. Big Ben was hung up on Lillian. Big Ben had a girl. Everyone figured it was funny, right? I remember how he was always making mistakes around then, not thinking even as well as he could if he tried. Ready was worried, he takes care of Wheeler. Lillian was playing with Ben. I remember how he hung around her like some puppy. Then I remembered how she'd been swearing at him lately, how bad he'd looked, hurt. I saw her laugh at him.''

He finished his wine now. He didn't go on.

"Wheeler was here that night?''

"Yes, in the cellar. In and out of the cellar entrance. No

trouble getting to her car in the lot. He often helped with the lot, no one'd even notice him out there. Like scenery.''

"Jack Ready was with him."

"Not all the time."

"You suspected all along?"

"Hell, no. Dobson was the victim, right? I didn't think about Lillian and Wheeler, why should I? Only after you came and talked to the bartender, when I realized it was Lillian the bomb was meant for, did I think about poor Ben.''

"How bad is he? He was in the Army."

"A Silver Star; killed twenty and saved ten of our own. I don't know how bad the shrinks would say. Dull, dumb, but enough brain to take care of himself ordinarily, enough to just barely make the Army. Jack Ready once told me Ben scored one point higher than absolute minimum to get in the Army. Slow, dumb, leaned on Ready for anything more than eating and washing himself, but not stupid, no sir.''

"Smart enough to plan the bombing, and smart enough to know he was too dumb to plan a decent alibi somewhere else?"

"Just about that smart. If he tried to get clever, get at her somewhere else, Ready would've been sure to suspect, and Wheeler might blow it, anyway."

"What did he do in the Army?"

"Demolition. He's a bomb man, right?"

"Where do I find him? Is he here?"

"No, he's off now. He lives with Ready out in a cabin just east of town. Foothill Road. Number 1270."

I stood up.

"Shaw," Vasto said, "take it easy on him, right? He's just a big dog, no real nastiness in him. But be careful. He is like a big dog, scared and always nervous. He's got guns, he can use them, and he's got to be jumpy, right?''

I nodded. I'd be very careful. The sheriff might be a good idea, but I didn't have any real proof yet, just Vasto's background and my own guesses. A horde of police could send a man like Wheeler off the deep end, turn him crazy violent, and maybe we never would know for sure. The best way was to go out there with Jack Ready, yes.

Except that when I went out, Jack Ready wasn't there at the table. He wasn't anywhere. I hurried to my car.

33

FOOTHILL ROAD WOUND in sharp switchbacks through the forest and the slopes of the lower Coast Range. The night was dark. I drove carefully, making as much time as I could. I met no other cars, and took one wrong turn before my headlights picked out the number 1270 on a mailbox at the side of the twisting road.

Number 1274 was across from it, and another house a few hundred feet on had lights in it. That made me feel better. There were people around. I drove on past the mailbox of number 1270 in case Ben Wheeler was in the cabin and had seen my lights. I pulled off the road into a grove of pines.

Working my way back along the silent night road—you can stumble too easily in unknown woods—I saw that there was light in the cabin at number 1270. As I reached the driveway that led to the cabin, I saw the two cars parked in it. One was a relatively recent Pontiac, the other was a battered old Ford. I recognized the Ford—the car that had tried to run me down at the Redwood Inn. Now I was sure.

Too sure. I walked up the driveway past the two cars, and the giant shadow loomed up to my left in the light from the cabin. I saw the arm come up—an arm that looked like some slow, enormous tree branch in the shadowy light of the dark night. I dived for cover. The shot was like thunder in the night. Something whispered past over where I lay sprawled in the leaves and bushes.

Three more shots sprayed wildly, going right and left and high up where all it could have hit was some owl.

I struggled my revolver out.

I didn't fire.

He was already running. Without a shot fired at him. Away from the driveway and the cabin, deeper into the thick forest, crashing and tearing branches like some great bear running in panic from a forest fire. Blind panic without a shot fired, just as he had done in the old Ford in the Redwood Inn parking lot. Low on the still night air I could almost hear a soft, hopeless moaning above the noise of his wild flight through the trees and brush.

I ran after him.

The tree branches and brush whipped at my face and legs. I swore, slowed down. It wouldn't help me to run head-on into a tree. Slower and steadier, let him fall and stumble in panic. I wasn't going to lose him as long as he was moving, the sound of his escape as loud as a bull elephant charging through a thick jungle.

I slowed to a steady trot, missing the heavier branches and thicker brush now that my eyes were accustomed to the dark under the tall trees. The noise of his progress veered right and left without pattern, and I got steadily closer. He was stumbling in a wide circle that was taking us farther from the cabin but not as far as it should have if he had run in a straight line. I felt like a hunter on the trail of an animal in panic, inexorably closing in on him no matter how hard he fought to escape. Bigger, stronger, but no match for me in the end. Heart and fear against implacable stalking.

Then the noise of his flight was gone. He had stopped. Somewhere ahead in the night. The animal run to ground, and far more dangerous that way.

I stopped, too. Listened. Something cracked in the brush not too far ahead. I listened, strained, and almost heard his heavy breathing. Did I hear it? Crouched out there, his eyes wide with panic, his heart pounding in his massive chest, his breathing hard and in gasps.

Yes. Maybe a hundred feet. Ahead and left. I stepped slowly, carefully, trying to remember Vietnam and how it was done. How you approached a waiting enemy in the dripping jungle so thick it was like an ocean from above. I was long out of practice, but I tried to move in silence. Move and listen at the same time.

I listened too hard.

Straining to hear any sound ahead in the dark trees, any movement, my feet stepped automatically—and stepped into empty air.

Falling, my arms flung out, and something hard and soft hit me in the face. Something loose and wet and then hard, and I lay stunned. Dazed. Without breath.

I lay without moving.

How long? I didn't know.

I was sitting up in the dark and silent night and looking up to the indistinct edge of the small gulley I had stepped into and fallen to the bottom where the leaves were thick and damp. I pawed for my pistol. My time to panic. I found my gun. I sat in the little gulley and looked up at the dark edge against the faintly lighter sky. I waited.

How long had I been stunned?

Had I been unconscious at all?

Where was he? Ben Wheeler? The terrified giant out there in the night running from me? Where was he now? Near? Just out of sight waiting for me to come up out of the gulley? Had heard me fall, and came with his gun to wait there, close, for me to show myself?

I heard the car motor. Behind and to my right. Where the cabin should be. An old motor, rough and coughing, and then the crunch of tires in gravel and the motor fading.

Wheeler? Or someone else? I had to find out.

Slowly, I stood up, raised my head above the edge of the small gulley. A feeling no one but a soldier, a policeman, or a criminal knows—raising your head up into possible sudden death. Like pushing your head, your will, against a massive weight that presses down on you.

Nothing happened. Nothing moved in the night. There was no sound in the forest. I stood up out of the gulley.

You know when there is no one near.

I began to trot back toward the cabin. After some minutes I saw its light off to the left. I came out of the woods at the edge of the driveway. The Pontiac was there, but the old Ford was gone. I went into the lighted cabin.

Inside it was bare and Spartan, the necessities and nothing more. Three small rooms and a kitchen. Little food or cooking equipment in the kitchen, Ready and Wheeler would eat most of their meals at The Pines. The tiny living room offered nothing. One bedroom had a bureau filled with sleek shirts, cuff links, and bright-colored socks. A closet full of colored slacks and three-toned sports coats. Jack Ready's room. The second bedroom could have belonged in a monastery.

A king-size bed that sagged in the middle; a bare bureau; no mirrors; a single chair; a closet with one suit, a heavy mackinaw, a pair of muddy boots, and some work pants. The bureau drawers held two changes of underwear, two denim shirts, the Silver Star medal in its lined box with the citation, and five snapshots of Lillian Marsak.

It was the first time I had seen the dead woman. I held the photos. She had been a dark woman, not tall but with the feeling of largeness. Full and slim and curved. An odd smile, and soft, hot eyes. Neither very young nor really beautiful, but with a sense of both alive youthfulness and the kind of beauty you remember alone in the dark later.

Two of the snapshots had been cut in half, as if some other man had been with her, had brought out the enigmatic smile, and Ben Wheeler had cut him out. In one picture, the most bent and handled, she wore only underwear, and her eyes were distant. I had the feeling that all the photos had been taken secretly, stolen when she wasn't looking. I put them back in the drawer. They were too much of a look into the anguished mind of a sad man.

Where was the driver of the Pontiac?

I went out of the empty house and around it. I saw nothing. I went down to the Pontiac. It was empty. There was no registration in the glove compartment. The other houses through the trees were still alight. No one had come out to investigate the shots earlier. It probably wasn't wise out here, and shots in the night might not have been uncommon.

I circled the cabin again, saw the dark shadow off in the trees to the rear. A narrow trail leading that way. The dark shape at the end of the trail was a small shack, without light or windows. A toolshed. Its door hung open on loose hinges. I went in, found a light switch among spider webs and the accumulated dirt of years.

Sticks of dynamite, a box of fuse caps, a tangle of wire littered an unpainted wooden table.

I found the driver of the Pontiac.

Jack Ready lay on the shack floor behind the table of bomb materials. In a pool of still-wet blood.

He was warm, and dead. I didn't have to listen to his heart or see if he breathed. No one could have breathed with half his head crushed, a deep gash in his chest. Ready had been stabbed, battered on the head like an eggshell. It could almost have been the work of some savage animal tearing at the terrierlike man. Tearing the purple-and-yellow jacket, the purple slacks and yellow suede shoes.

I went all around that shack. All I found was a bloody, long-handled ax with a dull blade, and a bloody hunting knife with a rusty ten-inch blade.

Had Jack Ready made a mistake? Heard Vasto and me in the office at The Pines, and come to warn Ben Wheeler? Warn him, and try to make him surrender, turn himself in? Or had the dull brain exploded into darkness needing no reason to lash out but fear itself? Maybe we'd never know.

I went back to the cabin. There was no telephone. Out in the night I looked along the road. No telephone poles.

I walked toward my car. There would be a telephone not too far away.

34

Sheriff Quigley looked down at the body. "You went off on your own, Shaw. Why?"

"All I had was a hunch," I said. "At first just a hunch that Lillian Marsak was the real target. Then I thought that if I moved fast I could catch the killer by surprise. If I came and told you I was afraid we'd lose the edge, send the killer under cover."

"You were wrong," Quigley said.

"Maybe, but what did I really have until I talked to Vasto tonight?"

Quigley thought for a time, his quiet eyes still fixed toward the dead Jack Ready. "You were wrong. We'll forget it. Anything in this shack? The cabin?"

"Not that I saw."

"Okay," Quigley said. "Doctor."

A beefy man with sleepy eyes ambled out of the pack of deputies behind Quigley and me. He carried a black bag, bent down over the dead man. The coroner's office man— Quigley was the coroner, of course.

"This won't be a hard job, will it?" Quigley said to the

back of the beefy doctor, turned to his deputies. "Two of you go over this shack, the body, and the grounds around it. You want anything that doesn't grow. The other two of you do the same in the cabin and around it. Shaw."

He led me back to the cabin, into the living room, and sat down with a mild groan. He had been in bed.

"Sit down and tell me all about it again."

I told him about it—from the moment the bartender at The Pines had made me realize that Dobson had picked up Lillian Marsak to my chase through the woods here for Ben Wheeler.

"You saw Wheeler?" Quigley asked.

"No, not exactly. A big man. The shadows can be deceptive, though. You think it was someone else?"

"No, I don't, but I'm ready to consider anything."

"You questioned Walt Sobers today. When did you decide it was Lillian Marsak the killer wanted, after all?"

"When Tom Allen came in about noon and told me about your questioning him and Cynthia Dobson. It took him a while, but he finally understood what Dobson's phone call to him that night had meant—a pickup."

"There all the time, no one saw it. None of them thought, just assumed it had to be Dobson the killer wanted."

"I assumed it, too, and so did you," Quigley said. "What else would anyone have thought? It's easy to know the answers once you know the right questions. We all saw what we expected."

"Except Campbell Grant."

"I'll have a long talk with Grant in a few days. There might even be a charge, not that I'll make it stick." He let out a weary sigh. "An accident, Russ Dobson getting killed. You never know, do you? Maybe the State Park rises and falls on an accident."

"It's a chancy world."

"Yeh."

He watched his two men going over the cabin. I didn't think they would find much. Neither did Quigley. He watched them with morose eyes, yawned. It was late by now.

"With Vasto's testimony, Walter Sobers' and Grant's story of her six o'clock appointment, and the bomb materials out in that shack, we've got the case, I guess. Too bad. Ben Wheeler is just a poor dumb ox. Lillian Marsak probably led him a hell of a bad chase, twisted him inside out. Those pictures in there." Quigley seemed to be seeing dark corners in his own mind. "Why did he have to kill Jack Ready, though? Like brothers."

"Panic," I said. "The breaking point when I came out after him. Who knows what Ready tried to do?"

"Where can he go now?" Quigley said, as much to himself as to me. "Without Jack Ready, what does he do?"

"He's an animal now," I said. "Dangerous."

"Maybe, and maybe not. You can't know what a man like Ben Wheeler will remember. A man like that is scared of the unknown, the strange. Scared of the dark. He'll hide, hole up for the night somewhere."

"He took his car."

"He's not stupid, Shaw. A mistake to think he is. He can't think in concepts, but he can think well enough in a straight line with facts. Someone is after him. He can think well enough to know what he has to do about that. But he can't be clever, do the unexpected. No, he'll go somewhere he knows."

"With Jack Ready dead, who can tell us that?"

"Maybe Sal Vasto," Quigley said. "In the morning.

We won't find Wheeler tonight. We'll work on here,
maybe spot a lead to where he'd go. Not that we will.''

"Call me when you go to Vasto?''

"I'll call you.''

I drove home along the twisting mountain road, and
along the highway to the Redwood Inn. It had been a long
day. But not as long as tonight would be for Ben Wheeler.

35

SLEEP CAME HARD that night, and I woke up for good early. I called our Los Angeles office. Mildred was already in.

"He's still not out of danger, Paul," she said. "But the doctors seem more relaxed."

I told her all about what had happened in Fort Smith. It might help Delaney get well faster. He was an old hunter, and the answer would make him feel better. Then I called Maureen.

"How long will you be, darling?" Her voice was sleepy. She worked nights, after all.

"Not long now," I said. "How's the show?"

"Closing notice." Her voice was bitter. For a good actress, personal triumph is good, but the play is more important. "They just don't understand it. They can praise stars and musicals without taking any risk."

"Sorry, baby. Maybe one more day, then we'll go somewhere."

"Don't promise. Thayer will have a new case."

He probably would have. I told her I loved her, and hung up. I showered and shaved, dressed, and was on my way for some breakfast when the telephone rang. It was Quigley. They hadn't found a trace of Ben Wheeler, or any leads at the cabin. He would meet me at The Pines.

Salvatore Vasto had coffee and some Danish when I got to his office. Quigley was already eating. I joined him. I wondered what Ben Wheeler was eating this morning. Whatever it was, it was more than what Jack Ready would ever eat again.

"Ready should have known better," Salvatore Vasto said. "A man like Ben Wheeler is a time bomb, handle with real care. You better find him fast."

"I plan to try," Quigley said. "That box of fuse caps we found at his cabin was bought in a San Francisco store. They already identified Wheeler as the man who bought the caps over a month ago."

"He was gone a few days," Vasto said. "I remember that Jack Ready was worried."

"You think Ready knew what Wheeler was planning to do?" Quigley said.

"He had to know," I said.

"No," Vasto said, "I don't think he did. Not before it happened. He would have stopped Wheeler. It would have been tricky to stop Big Ben, but if Jack Ready had known, he'd have tried. To save Ben."

"What about the bomb material in that shack?" I said.

"My guess would be that Ben kept it hidden, had it out last night to make another bomb," Vasto said. "Ben isn't stupid, right? He wouldn't have let even Ready see that stuff. He went off alone to buy the caps, right?"

"He's stupid," I said. "It was a stupid, clumsy murder. If Russell Dobson hadn't happened to be killed too, it would have been solved in a day. Obvious, dumb and crazy."

"Crazy," Sheriff Quigley said, "but not so dumb. If

Vasto there hadn't remembered, I'm not so sure I'd ever have connected Ben Wheeler to Lillian Marsak. Dobson might not have been any break for Wheeler. Without all the fuss over Dobson, and you coming up here, Vasto might never have thought about Ben Wheeler. No one else seems to remember Wheeler was after Lillian Marsak for a girl friend.''

"Stupid or smart," Sal Vasto said, "this isn't getting him caught. Where is he, Quigley?''

"That's what we came to ask you," Sheriff Quigley said. "Where would he go? Relatives? Friends?''

"No relatives I know of, and the only friend he had was Jack Ready," Sal Vasto said. The roadhouse owner leaned back in his desk chair to think. "He never did anything much without Jack Ready. I guess that's why Lillian Marsak hit him so hard. He never had a woman, not that I know. Maybe it was the only time he'd ever reached out for a woman, and then he got slapped down. I don't think he ever really had a woman.''

"He must have done something, liked somewhere," Quigley said.

"Ready, his work here, and gambling. He liked to gamble.''

"Where?" Quigley said.

"Anywhere he could. Backroom games, poker parties. Sometimes he used to go up to the logger camps to shoot dice. That's right. The logger camps. Ben liked it up there.''

"Where else? Bars? Motels?''

"No, Ben never drank much. A beer now and then if Ready bought for him. Taverns where they gamble, yes.''

"That's all you can tell us?''

"He just worked for me, Sheriff," Vasto said. "If I were you, I'd try the logger camps, and gambling games.''

"We'll try them," Quigley said. "Thanks for the coffee."

"An advantage of owning a restaurant," Vasto said, smiling.

We drove back to Quigley's office in the courthouse. I sat in a corner while the sheriff set the wheels in motion. He pulled all the deputies he could from other work and sent them out to comb the area for gambling games. He sent them to the logging camps within twenty miles.

"I had the roads blocked this morning, every other way out," Quigley said. "We're fortunate in this county, only three ways out by road. I don't think Wheeler would try any other way but his car. Unless the bus, and we're watching."

"What can I do?"

"Nothing now. This is police work, routine plodding." He grinned at me. "You don't know the county. Go and take a walk in the redwoods, take a nap. I'll call you when we think we know something. All we do now is wait."

I went to find Nancy Cathcart. She was working in Dobson's office among stacks of boxes all tied with string. Boxes of books, papers, office supplies. All that was left of the work and life of Senator Russell Dobson—a roomful of boxes.

"Take a break," I said.

"You didn't come back last night." She tied a box.

"No. We found our bomber, Nancy."

She stopped tying the box, looked up. "Found? Who?"

"Come out for coffee, I'll tell you. Maybe a drink?"

"Tell me—!" She stopped. "Yes, I think a drink."

We went to a storefront bar down on the main street. At the morning hour it was almost empty. A single old woman and two young men in work clothes sat at the bar. We were the only ones at a table. Nancy ordered a Bloody Mary. Reserved in all things. It was probably the only

time she'd had a drink in the morning in her life. I ordered
Scotch. The bartender put them on the bar where I went
and got them.

"Tell me," Nancy said.

I told her. She said nothing for a time.

"Ben Wheeler?" she finally said. "No. Not poor Ben
Wheeler. He . . . he wanted Lillian Marsak?"

"So it seems," I said.

She drank, a long drink, and her eyes flashed at me.
"Men and women! Lying, cheating, stealing, killing! Is that
what we were meant for? Is that the way it is? Isn't any
man honest? Any woman devoted?"

"Given a chance, most are. Men and women," I said.
"Some never get a decent chance. The rest is in your
mind, Nancy. Your problem, not the world's."

She stared into her drink. "I wish you had come back
last night. I . . . I want to change. Try."

"I'm married."

"I know that, don't I?"

"Why not now, then?"

"No!" Color in her face, her mouth clamped. She took
a deep breath. "Tonight, Paul. In my own house."

"All right," I said. "If I can."

"I have to go back to work."

After she left I had another Scotch. I didn't often drink
in the morning, either, but I was thinking of Ben Wheeler,
hearing him crash through the trees and brush like a great
bear in terror last night. I was thinking of the pictures of
Lillian Marsak, and the pain of a big, dumb, slow man
who had tried to be her man. And I thought of that dead
farm back on Hill Road with the broken mother and bitter,
whining father. It was hard to know, sometimes, whom to
blame, whom to understand.

From the bar I drove to the beach. The afternoon was

clear and cool, the sun in winter light now. The change from late summer to early winter coming while I had been in Fort Smith. A chill settling over the land of giant shore rocks and tall redwoods. I wanted to go now, wanted it over. I couldn't walk on the beach, no. I drove back to the Redwood Inn.

There was no one to call, I didn't want to read. I lay on the bed and waited. I watched the ceiling of the room. I looked at the windows. I looked again at the windows, and it was dark. I sat up, my head thick. I had dozed. My watch said seven o'clock. I would have heard the telephone. I decided to eat.

A big meal. To pass the time. A steak, a crab cocktail, drinks, soup, dessert, coffee. The works. It passed two hours. Where the hell was Ben Wheeler? There were questions I had to ask, answers I had to have.

I went back to my room, decided to shave again, and the telephone rang. It was Sheriff Quigley.

"Come on," he said.

36

I RODE WITH Quigley. The car of deputies came behind us. It was a short drive. Into the redwoods, the sea off to our right as we drove south. A winter sea now, suddenly, with that angry roll of noise like a constant, rumbling bass. We left the highway and turned onto a logging road, and even the stars vanished beneath the giant trees towering too high for me to see their tops.

The logging camp was less than three miles from Fort Smith. A base camp with more or less permanent barracks and a cookhouse. Sheriff Quigley stopped his cars before we entered the camp itself.

"Stay out here, cover the road," he told his deputies. "I don't want a shoot-out. Shaw and I'll go in alone on foot. Be alert. Wheeler's a gentle man unless he panics again. If he does, don't try to stop him by muscle. Shoot."

The sheriff and I walked on into the camp.

"He's hiding here? Two of us to dig him out?"

"Not hiding," Quigley said. "Visiting. The camp boss told us Wheeler doesn't act like he's got a worry in the world. He ate chow with the loggers, just hanging around."

"He's forgotten? Mind slipped?"

"Could be. I've seen it happen with smarter men. The mind forgets what it has to forget, sometimes."

Men in work clothes walked around the trampled dirt of the logging camp. They paid no attention to us. Equipment and tools were parked and piled everywhere without any apparent pattern. Quigley walked slowly, his gun not in sight, looking into barracks and tents. Most of the buildings were almost empty, a few men lying around on bunks. Quigley stopped a man.

"Where's the game?" he asked.

"The toolshed. Last building down left."

It was a long, low building without windows. We went in and saw a light at the far end. Some fifteen men in work clothes and boots were gathered in a small tight circle, all staring down toward the floor at their center. They all held money in loose sheaves in their hands. As we walked up the money changed hands quickly and with few words. I didn't see Ben Wheeler.

The knot of men saw us approaching. They seemed to freeze where they were, the money suspended in midair on its way from hand to hand. Some of them began to sidle toward a rear side door. Money miraculously vanished.

"Relax," Sheriff Quigley said. "I'm not here for any gambling. You can go right on after I—"

I saw Ben Wheeler at the same moment. The loggers became aware of whom we were looking at. They parted like a herd of cattle before a horse and rider, opening to give us room.

"Hello, Ben," Quigley said. He made no move for his gun.

The big man was on his knees in the center of the circle. The man with the dice, the shooter. He grinned up at the sheriff. His eyes were dull, vacant, as if he knew the man

who had spoken to him, but couldn't place him. He knew
Quigley, but who was Quigley?

"Two points 'n' three passes in a row," Ben Wheeler
said, grinned at Quigley and all around, happy. "Shoot it
all. Take it all or any part. I'm coming out."

None of the loggers moved. No one laid down any
money. Ben Wheeler blinked up at them all.

"I'm shooting, come on," the big man said. "Keep it
goin'. I'm hot, real hot. Natural every time. Take your
lumps!"

Quigley said, "Shoot, Ben."

The loggers had begun to melt away. Despite the sheriff's assurance, they slipped quietly toward the side door
and the front door. Like the silent small animals of the
forest that sensed trouble. Ben Wheeler blinked at the dice
in his big hands, at the bare dirt floor where there was no
money, at the vanishing loggers. His face no longer smiling, happy.

"Put it down, you guys! Come on. Whatsa matter? I'm
too hot for you? What're you scared of? Shoot it all. Take
any part, I take all the action you got. Put it down!"

But he was talking to an empty shed. They were all
gone, quick and silent. Only Quigley and I stood there
over the massive man down on his knees with the dice in
his big hands, and a look of sorrow in his dull eyes. The
gamblers were gone. The game was over.

"Shoot, Ben," Quigley said.

The big man looked at the dirt. "I ain't covered."

"You're covered," I said, dropped twenty dollars onto
the dirt floor. "I'll take it all."

There was a silence in the empty shed. Then Ben Wheeler
grinned again. The game was on. He blew on the dice lost
in his fleshy hands. He shook them, his eyes dark and
intense. Rolled. Hunched forward eagerly, anxiously, as
the dice hit the wall, bounced back off, settled. Eleven.

"Natural!" Wheeler cried. "Four in a row! Ride it!"

He looked up at me, excited, his eyes half crazed now. Quigley bent and picked up the dice. He picked up my twenty, handed it to me. Ben Wheeler watched him.

"That's all, Ben," Quigley said. "Four in a row, a good ride. But the game's over. You're under arrest, Ben."

The big man said nothing, didn't move from where he still knelt in the dirt.

"For Lillian Marsak," Quigley said. "We know all about it now. Mr. Vasto told us. She treated you bad."

Wheeler licked his lips. "Mr. Vasto?"

"We know where you bought the fuse caps," Quigley said. "You had the dynamite all along, right? You made the bomb, planted it on her car that evening in The Pines parking lot. We know now it was Lillian you wanted to kill. There were witnesses, Ben. You were seen."

I heard the lie. A necessary lie. We knew, but Quigley was trying to tell it in terms that would make Ben Wheeler know that we had to know. Simple terms—you were seen, after all, Ben Wheeler. And Mr. Vasto told us.

"You thought she was your girl," Quigley said. "Then she dumped you, told you to go away. So you killed her."

The big man said, "My girl!"

His voice was thick, suddenly broken. He remembered. He looked up at the sheriff and knew who he was. He looked at me. He started to get up, and sat down in the dirt of the shed.

"My girl," Ben Wheeler said. "Lillian. She laughed."

"Give me your gun, Ben," Quigley said.

The big man sat. Then he reached a hand into his right coat pocket. I tensed, my hand on my own revolver. The big man handed his pistol up to the sheriff.

37

BEN WHEELER SAT there in the dirt of the logging toolshed. An empty shed, with only Quigley and me to hear him.

"She was my girl, you know? Me 'n' her, Lillian. Then they took her away. Them! She was my girl, on'y she changed. Money. She wanted money. Anyone asks, she takes 'em home. That guy Sobers works by Boetter's trucks. Some new guy. I seen what he give her. For her ears, real jewels. I call her. I try to see her. She won't talk to me no more. Get lost! I calls her old woman's place. She gets mad. She laughs at me! At me she got to laugh. Calls me 'n ape, laughs in my face."

Quigley moved, loosened his coat over his pistol, stepped a step closer to the big man. To break the mood, the big man getting worked up, reliving his rejection and sudden hate of Lillian Marsak. Hearing her laugh in his begging face. His girl. His face darkening.

"She was no good, Ben. I know that. I understand," Quigley said.

"No good," Ben Wheeler said, nodded there on the dirt floor. "I said I got to see her, see? I said I got to talk to her new guy. I made her mad, see?'' He looked up, cunning in his shallow eyes. "I already been down to Frisco, got the caps, fixed up the bomb out in the shed where Jack don't see. A bomb, that's the way. No one traces a bomb. A bomb—you ain't there when it goes off. I made her real mad. I know if I make her mad she'll come 'n' talk to me, tell me off. In the parkin' lot so no one thinks anything funny I'm there. I work fast, fix the bomb up, go back down the cellar. I know she ain't tellin' no one she's gonna meet with Ben Wheeler.''

Nothing is perfect, symmetrical, not even imperfection. He had a damaged brain, a slow brain, but there was a part of that brain that could function as well as any man's, and a part that could see and understand Lillian Marsak. Some part of his mind that saw clearly how Lillian Marsak viewed him—the ape, the dumb ox, not a man she wanted anyone to know she had once made love to even briefly. She wouldn't talk about meeting him, and she hadn't. One clear part of his brain, and there were others, but isolated, separated, not connected to each other.

"I heard it go off.'' He seemed to stare at a wall of the shed as if he saw the explosion there. "I didn't know he'd be with her. She was supposed to meet me, come alone. Why'd she bring that Dobson with her? I got nothin' against that Dobson.'' He shook his head almost sadly, agreeing with himself that he had nothing against Russell Dobson, one part of his mind talking to another. Then his small eyes flashed, a new voice in his head. "He got what was comin', that Dobson. He was goin' home with her, yeh. Anyone goes home with her. No-good bitch.''

He'd gone through a circle, the unconnected parts of his brain bringing him back to where he had started. She was still alive, Lillian Marsak. She went home with anyone. She was a no-good bitch. He hated her, he would kill her, he had to. His mind like a circle of slow fire with darkness all around, coming back on itself without beginning or end, without time beyond here and now, today, and he lived once more the hate that had made him make his bomb and use it.

"She was dead," I said, "and everyone thought it was Russell Dobson the bomb had been meant to kill. You were safe. But Campbell Grant came to Los Angeles to hire a detective. You followed him, shot the detective. You followed me, tried to have me shot. You had friends."

His massive head hung down. "Got no friends. Me 'n' Jack. He got lots o' friends, Jack got. Jack 'n' me."

Quigley said, "Ready got people to go down to Los Angeles? Ready had Shaw followed?"

"Follow?" Wheeler said, blinked in the weak light of that shed. "Mr. Vasto he sends us to bring that L.A. cop. I hear, sure. He come to find out, so I follow him, see? Jack says he handle it, I should hide low, but I follow. On'y he sees me by that motel 'n' I got to get away. I forget, the car goes backward, but I get away, sure. On'y he don't stop, he don't go away like Jack says. I make new bomb. I make good bombs. They showed me in the Army."

"You made a bomb, put it on my car," I said.

An anger crossed Wheeler's face like a small cloud in an empty sky. "Jack he come after me. Jack he sees me put the bomb on the L.A. cop's car. He's mad, he makes me go away. No more killin', he says. He makes me go away, 'n' he takes off the bomb from the L.A. cop's car. Jack, he shouldn't of done that. I know. I got to make that L.A. cop go away like Lillian. Jack he got no right takin' that bomb off."

The bomb on my car made more sense now. In broad daylight at a motel, only a Ben Wheeler would try something like that. Only because it had been Ben Wheeler would a Jack Ready have risked taking it off. For Ben Wheeler's sake.

"Is that why you killed Ready?" Sheriff Quigley said. "He was stopping you, said 'no more killing'? He told you to come and turn yourself in last night?"

"Jack 'n' me," Ben Wheeler said, nodded, and then, slowly, stared up at both of us. "Jack? You get Jack, he got to tell me what I should do, see?"

"Jack's dead, Ben," Quigley said. "You killed him last night. In the shack. You remember."

Ben Wheeler stared. "Dead? Jack ain't dead. You're crazy. Jack knows what I got to do."

"He's dead, Ben. Last night. You hit him with an ax, stabbed him with a knife. After you shot at Shaw," Quigley said.

"You're a dirty liar!" Wheeler cried out.

"Jack's dead," Quigley said. "He knew Mr. Vasto had told Shaw about you, went out to the cabin to make you give up. You—"

"Dead?" Wheeler said.

Maybe I should have seen it. That flash in the big man's cloudy eyes, but it's hard for the normal brain to work with the abnormal. Assumption again, the complex of fixed ideas, preconceived notions, that make up all our brains. The so-called rational mind has trouble following the irrational mind. The unexpected twists of a damaged brain take us by surprise.

"Jack, he ain't dead, no," Wheeler said. "You get Jack."

Quigley shook his head. "He was killed last night, Ben. Out at your cabin. I'm sorry. Okay—"

I moved in to help the big man to his feet, and that was when he jumped. One instant he was sitting there on the dirt floor, limp and hunched and broken, and the next he was up like some big cat and on me.

Lightning for such a big man, in a single motion of his legs and massive body. His eyes with that clear flash of sudden intelligence.

His fist hit my jaw and I was down, sprawled flat as a tree going over.

Through a haze of slow motion I saw and could do nothing.

Quigley had his gun out. Alert for it, ready, his gun out as fast as the big man had moved. Aimed straight at Wheeler in silence, no time to make a sound.

Wheeler ran straight at the sheriff. A tank in motion.

Quigley shot.

In suspended slow motion, Quigley shot, Wheeler lumbered straight on, the gun flew in a light-catching arc through the air of the shed, Quigley was down on his back, Wheeler ran over him as if he were no more than part of the dirt floor.

Quigley's head jerked back as Wheeler's boot hit his chin, lay stunned on that floor, and Wheeler ran on for the open side door and out into the night, his bloody left leg dragging like a dead thing.

38

"HOW FAR CAN he get, Chief?" a deputy said. "We found him this time okay."

"It took almost twenty-four hours this time," I said, "and he was in some kind of shock, had made himself forget. This new escape is something else. He knows now. He's out of his shock, and he remembers. He's shot and in pain and he knows."

Quigley and I had both been down on the dirt floor for some minutes, the big man gone, the night silent. Stunned, we hadn't moved. In a kind of shock, both of us. When the deputies finally came running, brought by the single shot from Quigley's gun, we got to our feet like sleepwalkers, neither of us speaking for a time. The sheriff picked up his gun, wiped off the dirt. I just stood and lit a cigarette.

Now the shed was full of deputies and loggers crowded all around us. Other deputies and loggers were out in the forest, alert for danger, but finding neither danger nor Ben Wheeler.

"He won't get far now that he's shot," Quigley said.

"Not in those woods. Maybe he'll go into that shock again, forget what happened again. He can't hold anything in his mind too long. I'll send for more men. We'll search the woods in force, but it's my hunch that we don't really have to do anything. Sooner or later he'll just walk out to us himself."

"He doesn't have his gun any more," I said.

"There's that at least," Quigley said. "What made him flip out that way, Shaw? You know?"

"Jack Ready being dead, I think. Too much for him to take."

"Yeh, I made a mistake there. Being reminded that he killed Jack Ready was way too much for his mind to take."

"He knows now, though," I said. "I saw his eyes. He really knows. I don't think he'll forget Ready now."

"Maybe not, but he'll come in and surrender. His nerves won't take it alone too long. He's shot and in pain. He's a child, mentally, and now that he's hurt he'll forget everything and look for help."

It was one of the deputies who brought the bad news. Ben Wheeler hadn't forgotten it all yet, wasn't acting now like a child in pain. And he wasn't out there alone in the woods.

"His car's gone," the deputy said. "One of the loggers showed me where it'd been. He must have circled around and drove it off. There was blood on the ground, but not much."

Quigley said, "Go get the roadblocks back up. Watch all ways out of the damned county again. I want him fast!"

The deputies went off to work. The loggers drifted away. Quigley and I were alone.

"He won't get far," Quigley said again, reassuring himself.

"Won't he? This time he knows Jack Ready's dead, he's got nowhere to go around here. He could be out of the county already, Quigley."

"I'll send out a bulletin."

"I guess there's nothing I can do now."

"Nothing. It's over."

For everyone except Ben Wheeler, and that was only a matter of time.

I drove back to the Redwood Inn. Nancy Cathcart said she would be waiting for me at her house. I didn't care now. I was tired. Tomorrow I would drive back to Los Angeles, and then fly home to Maureen. I had my woman. Fort Smith was already behind me. I went to bed.

39

AFTER BREAKFAST, I packed up. Technically, Nancy Cathcart owed me money, but it was only technical. John Thayer could chalk up the expenses of this one to overhead—for Delaney. I didn't want to call Nancy Cathcart, and she hadn't called me. Two nights of not showing up would be too much even for her.

I was all packed and ready when Tom Allen, Cynthia Dobson and Campbell Grant knocked at my door. They came in together. An unusual team. Cynthia Dobson thanked me for solving the death of her brother.

"I feel I should pay you something," Campbell Grant said. "You did the work, Quigley says there's no need to bring me into it at all."

"I'll take it. Three hundred will do."

Grant sat down to write out the check. John Thayer would be delighted. It's good to work for your partner, necessary, but money is better.

"What happens now?" I said to Tom Allen. "In politics."

The blond young man shrugged. "It's hard to be sure

yet. Ben Wheeler isn't going to be any part of politics. A poor slob hung up on a woman. People will relax some."

"Poor Ben," Cynthia Dobson said. "And poor Russ. To die by mistake, just chance."

"Will it help you, Allen?" I asked. "Dobson's death not political at all?"

"No," Allen said. "It won't help me."

Campbell Grant stood up, gave me the check. I took it.

"It has to help in the long run," Grant said. The tall lawyer glanced at Tom Allen. "People have to feel guilty in time about what they thought of Tom and his ecology people. Give them some time, modify the stand some, and who knows?"

"Changing sides again, Grant?" I said. I looked at Tom Allen. "A compromise? Bring Grant in with you?"

"Jesse Boetter and MacGruder will win for sure," the young radical candidate said. "Dobson's gone, but the murder wasn't political, so the boycott won't happen, no recall. Boetter will get most of Dobson's votes now. You have to compromise to win against MacGruder and Boetter. Not this time, but maybe next time with Grant in our corner and a softer line."

"And Grant the candidate instead of you," I said. "A safer image."

"I'm not so ambitious," Allen said. "The park counts."

"The trees are what matters," Cynthia Dobson said.

"Besides, you'll get all your money and your brother's," I said. "You can start that study center, and live well, too."

"A study center is a good thing here," Campbell Grant said. The opportunist, preparing his new role already. MacGruder had probably talked to him. With all the trouble over, Jesse Boetter a shoo-in now, MacGruder had no more need for Campbell Grant in the wings. A practical man, MacGruder. Grant had to change sides, there was nowhere else to go, and if I were MacGruder I'd keep an eye on Grant for the future. Still, if I had to bet, I'd put my money on Sam MacGruder all the way.

After they had gone, I carried my bag down to the car, paid my bill and drove out onto the highway and south. The redwoods still towered to the right. They had been there a long time—as long as the beach almost, and only a little less long than the darkness outside the circle of fire. I wondered how much longer they would be there in the winter light.

I stopped at the roadblock on the county line. The deputies were stopping every car. When they recognized me, they waved me on. I stopped, anyway.

"Not caught yet?" I said to a deputy.

"No trace yet."

"Then he's got to be out of the county."

"Sheriff says no," the deputy said. "We found his car early this morning. Near the beach. Blood in a culvert. He must have slept there. Tracks led off up the beach into the State Park. He's on foot now, nowhere near getting out of the county."

There were cars behind me. I drove on south. For a mile. Then I pulled off the highway, turned, and headed back.

40

SHERIFF QUIGLEY DOODLED on a memo pad on his desk.

"He's still around Fort Smith," I said.

"It looks that way," Quigley said.

I sat facing the sheriff in his office. My bag was still packed in my car outside the courthouse.

"He could have gotten out, gotten away. He had his car, your roadblocks wouldn't have been in operation again in time if he'd wanted to drive straight out of the county."

"I guess he could have," Quigley agreed. "If a man like Ben Wheeler could think straight, logically. He can't. You saw it, Shaw. He killed his only friend, and he didn't even know he was dead. He really didn't remember."

"Maybe he really didn't know," I said.

Quigley doodled. "You're saying there might be someone else? Ben Wheeler didn't kill Lillian Marsak and Dobson?"

"No, he killed them, but I'm not so sure he killed Jack Ready."

"You're letting your emotions get in the way, Shaw,"

the sheriff said. "You're sorry for Wheeler, you want to help. I'm sorry for him, too, but it can't change anything."

"Why is he staying around the county? He should run."

"Why would anyone else kill Jack Ready? What motive?"

I lit a cigarette, leaned toward him. "The man who shot my partner was a professional, probably black. The two who came after me were pros, I know that. Would Ben Wheeler hire professionals? Could he?"

"Jack Ready did that. Ready had two convictions down in San Francisco before he came here—one for extortion, one for bookmaking. He had the connections, yes. Wheeler set his bomb off, Jack Ready found out afterward. Then he went to work to protect Big Ben."

"Then why would Wheeler kill Ready? His only help?"

"Who knows why? Maybe we'll never know. By now Wheeler himself probably doesn't know. He's irrational, a violent man when scared or confused. He confuses easily, could do almost any violence. You figured all that out yourself."

"I know, last night. But all of a sudden I feel that something isn't right, damn it."

"Jack Ready made some mistake, scared Ben. Maybe Ben was making another bomb, Ready got mad and Ben lashed out. It fits the killing. A wild swing of that ax. Two more swings, and the knife. Berserk. We know he killed Lillian and Russ Dobson."

"Lillian, yes," I said. I was up. I walked around in that small office. "It's Dobson that bothers me. Dobson and his date with Lillian Marsak. Just that night. And Wheeler staying here when he should be five hundred miles away and still running."

"Ben is irrational, Shaw. Dobson picked up Lillian

Marsak that evening. For God's sake, man, you proved that yourself.''

I walked. ''Why did she let him pick her up?''

''If you'd known Lillian Marsak, you wouldn't ask. She liked men too much. Too many of them.''

''Except that she had Campbell Grant. Her big chance. She was closing her past. She'd given walking papers to Walt Sobers, her steady man. She wanted Ben Wheeler gone for good. Why turn around and let a casual one-night stand pick her up? And the one man in Fort Smith who might talk to Campbell Grant?''

Quigley doodled. ''I can't answer that. Too many things drive people. We don't always do what is logical, best for us.''

He was right, I had to admit it. I wasn't even sure just what I had in mind, except that Ben Wheeler had some reason for staying in Fort Smith.

''You're saying Ben Wheeler knows something we don't?'' Quigley said. ''Plans to do something more?''

''I think he has a reason to stay here.''

''I think you're wrong. He's just scared, confused.''

''I hope you're right,'' I said.

41

THE GRAY-HAIRED receptionist in Campbell Grant's elegant office squawked as I went past her without stopping. She was right behind me as I walked in on Grant. He stood up behind his desk when he saw me.

"Shaw?"

There was surprise in his voice, and something like alarm, too. That could have been just because he sensed that my being back had to mean some kind of trouble. He nodded sharply to the gray-haired lady clucking behind me. She left, outraged by both of us.

"What is it, Shaw?" Campbell Grant said.

"I'm not sure," I said. "Some questions."

I sat down, forming my thoughts. After a moment Grant sat down too. He was wary, but wouldn't I have been if someone like me had come barging in when all had seemed over?

I said, "That night at the beach place, when we talked about you and Lillian Marsak, you said something."

"Said what?"

"You said Lillian wouldn't have let Russell Dobson

pick her up. You said she'd stopped going with any man who asked her, she wanted you. I didn't believe you, but you insisted. You couldn't explain what had happened, but you were sure she wouldn't have let Dobson pick her up.''

"Yes, I remember. She wouldn't have."

"You said there had to be some explanation. Have you maybe thought of one?"

"No, I haven't," he said. "I've tried not to think about her at all. After you proved it was Ben Wheeler who set that bomb, I wanted to forget."

"Can you?"

"No, but I will," he said. His face was pale now. "I'm not exactly a nice guy. It's a tough world, you get what you can grab. I never gave a damn about other people, but I gave a damn about Lillian, and I'm not going to forget easily. But I will forget. I'll do it."

"But you can't explain why she let Dobson pick her up?"

"I know she wouldn't have. But she did."

"She wanted you. You were her chance. To let Russell Dobson pick her up wasn't logical. Inconsistent."

"Perhaps she wasn't being logical," Grant said.

"Let's say she was logical. Let's try an explanation, at least a partial one," I said. "Let's say she *didn't* let Dobson pick her up—not exactly. She went with him, took him with her that evening, but not for the usual reason. Not what we all assumed. Not a date, not sex, not a big evening man to woman. Some other reason."

"What reason?" Grant was alert, chewed at his lip.

"That I don't know yet, but say there was a reason we can't see. There has to be. You're right, Grant. She wouldn't have risked letting Dobson, or anyone else, pick her up. So why?"

Grant was watching me. "Does it matter why? Whatever her reason, she risked losing me, anyway. How could I have told what her reason was? It would have looked like a regular pickup to me, right? Sex and a big night with Dobson."

"Unless she knew she could explain it to you later," I said. "Or unless she did it for you."

A few seconds is a long time when a question is hanging in the air. Grant seemed to be hoping the question would go away.

"Why would I want her to let Dobson pick her up?"

"Some plan to compromise Dobson? Pressure? Work more or less with Tom Allen and Cynthia Dobson to force Dobson out of the campaign? You take his place?"

"No," Campbell Grant said. "I had no plan."

"Maybe not," I said. I got up to leave. "They haven't caught Ben Wheeler yet. It's funny, but he hasn't run away, he's still around Fort Smith. I wonder why?"

Grant said nothing.

"He should have run far and fast," I said.

"Should he have?" Grant said.

That was all.

42

Sam MacGruder had Jesse Boetter with him in his office. The head of the Lumbermen's Association and his candidate were in conference when I walked in on them. They looked pleased with themselves. MacGruder even smiled at me. Boetter didn't.

"You did nice work, Shaw," Sam MacGruder said. "Who'd have figured on Big Ben?"

"They let guys like that run loose," Jesse Boetter said. "I'd lock 'em up, throw away the key. Maybe I'll run a bill like that through the senate."

"You figure you're in now?" I said. "Home free?"

MacGruder laughed. "No trouble at all now. Dobson's out of the way, Allen's already lost the timid liberals, and with Ben Wheeler the killer we come out clean. Win in a walk."

"You don't even need Campbell Grant in reserve."

"Save money that way," MacGruder said.

"He's gone over to Tom Allen."

"Yeh, that figures. He's got to go somewhere," Boetter said.

"No worries about Grant?"

"When the time comes, I'll think about it," MacGruder said.

"Any worries about Ben Wheeler?" I said. "He's hanging around Fort Smith. He could have been in Mexico, maybe. I wonder why he's staying here?"

Jesse Boetter said, "Here? Wheeler's still around?"

"Hurt, desperate, and still here."

MacGruder said, "You've got something on your mind?"

"Something," I said. "That telephone call Russell Dobson got in your office here that afternoon. You're sure there was a telephone call?"

MacGruder's eyes were flint. "I'm sure."

"No one's sure just why Dobson went to The Pines that evening. Bad coincidence," I said. "Maybe someone wanted him to go there?"

"So?" MacGruder said.

"Someone could have arranged to meet him there, right? That telephone call—if there was a call."

"I said there was," MacGruder said.

"Boetter there wasn't with you that afternoon, was he?"

"I was in my office working, Shaw," Jesse Boetter said.

"Yeh," I said. "You said that call was a woman, MacGruder?"

"That's what I said."

"She didn't say who she was, and you didn't know the voice?"

"That's it."

I nodded. "When Dobson talked on the telephone, did it sound like he was talking to a woman? A social call?"

Sam MacGruder seemed to think. "I don't know. No, come to think of it, it didn't sound like that. More like business, a man on the other end. Can't be sure, but it had the sound.''

"The woman maybe a secretary? Calling for her boss, and when Dobson took the phone he talked to the boss?''

"Could be," MacGruder agreed.

"But he said nothing about The Pines? About the phone call?''

"Nothing," MacGruder said.

"It couldn't have been Lillian Marsak who called," I said slowly, "she just happened to meet Dobson at that bar. But it could have been someone getting him to The Pines.''

Jesse Boetter said, "What the hell are you cooking up now, Shaw? The whole thing's finished, ended.''

"Maybe it is," I said. "But it looks like Ben Wheeler doesn't think so.''

"Why would that be?" Sam MacGruder asked.

"I guess we'll have to ask Wheeler that when we get him," I said. "Won't we?''

43

IT WAS LUNCHTIME when I reached The Pines, the parking lot full of cars. The dining room and bar were equally full of businessmen. Salvatore Vasto wasn't among them. The roadhouse owner was in his office as usual. As I went in I had the sudden realization that I had never seen Vasto anywhere else. He was eating a sandwich.

"I didn't expect to see you again," he said, putting the sandwich down carefully.

I had seen him work here, eat here, drink here. As if he never lived anywhere else, had no life outside this office, his roadhouse. Where did he sleep?

"You're not married, Vasto?" I said.

He wiped his fingers with a napkin. "I'm married. If you want to call it that."

"You don't live here?"

"Here?" he said. "No, I've got a home. A good home, cost me plenty. I'm a Catholic, Shaw. The old-country ways, right? You marry, you stay married no matter what. My wife is a good Catholic, right?"

"A marriage you don't work at, but a marriage?"

"That's how it works sometimes. You came around to talk about my marriage?"

"I came to talk about why Russell Dobson was here in your place that night," I said. "I mean, why was he here at all? You said he didn't come to your place much. Real bad luck for him he happened to be here just that evening."

"I guess it was," Vasto agreed.

"Unless someone got him here that day," I said. "Set him up. Telephoned him at Sam MacGruder's office and arranged for Dobson to come here."

"Why would anyone do that?"

"Maybe to make sure he was with Lillian Marsak in that car when the bomb went off."

Vasto was no fool, he understood what I was saying at once. He pushed his sandwich away, wiped at his fingers again, his mouth.

"Someone set him up? Dobson was the victim, after all?"

"They were both targets, maybe," I said, "but of two different killers. Ben Wheeler planted the bomb to kill Lillian Marsak, but someone else sent Russell Dobson to get killed."

"By getting him here?" Vasto said, and thought for a while. "How could this 'maybe' second killer know Lillian Marsak would be picked up by Dobson? How would anyone know Dobson would pick her up?"

"Dobson was a known chaser. It was a good chance."

"Chancy, though," Vasto said, thought some more. "And this second killer must have known that Ben Wheeler was going to plant a bomb to kill Lillian Marsak. The second party must have known what Wheeler was going to do. That doesn't seem very reasonable, right?"

"Maybe not," I had to agree. "Can I talk to that bartender again? Marco?"

Vasto pressed his button. A stranger came in—Jack Ready and Ben Wheeler both gone. Vasto told the new man to get the bartender. Neither of us had anything to say while we waited. The bartender came in.

"Tell me about Dobson and Lillian Marsak again," I said. "All of it you remember."

He did. Lillian Marsak had come in first at five o'clock. Ginny Piper had been with her. Russell Dobson came in later, sat alone. Ginny Piper had left. The next thing the bartender knew, Dobson and Lillian Marsak were together. Dobson made his call to Tom Allen, and he and Lillian went out together to her car just before six o'clock.

"Did you hear anything Dobson and Lillian said to each other?" I asked.

"Not much," Marco said. "Pickup talk, long time no see, like that. He thought she'd forgotten him. She said he'd been a stranger to her place, maybe they should fix that. He said her place sounded cozy. The usual malarkey."

I frowned. "It sounds as if she were enticing him to go with her. *She* suggested her place?"

"Well, sort of, I guess. It's hard to say exactly, you know? I mean, it's all kind of jockeying around. But I guess that's about how it sounded, yeh."

"Did Dobson mention anyone else? Maybe ask if someone was looking for him? Leave a message for anyone? Ask if anyone had asked for him that evening? Act as if he might have come here to meet someone else?"

"No," Marco said. "He didn't say nothing like that."

"All right, Marco," I said. "Thanks."

The bartender left. Salvatore Vasto picked up his sandwich, started to eat. I watched him.

"It sounds like *she* could have been doing the enticing," I said. "She suggested going to her place."

"You can't be sure," Vasto said thoughtfully as he

chewed his sandwich. "Like Marco said, Shaw, in a
pickup everyone is sort of playing a game, right? Titillat-
ing each other."

"Yes," I agreed. "But I think someone got Dobson
here that evening, arranged for him to meet Lillian Marsak.
I think Ben Wheeler knows that somehow, that's why
Wheeler is still around Fort Smith. He's looking for whoever got Dobson here that evening."

"Ben?" Vasto said, chewing. "Around here?"

"Yes," I said. "He should be running, but he's not.
He's hiding here, taking a big chance."

"Why would Ben care who got Dobson here, if anyone
did?"

"Because whoever got Dobson here that evening killed
Jack Ready later. Or Big Ben thinks so."

"You don't believe Ben killed Jack Ready himself?"

"I think that someone set Russell Dobson up for that
bomb, Vasto, and Jack Ready could have known who it
was."

"Why? I mean, why would someone do that? Motive?"

"I don't know," I said. "When I do know, then I'll
know who did it, won't I?"

"Yeh, I guess that'd do it, right?"

He finished his sandwich, wiped his mouth.

44

I FOUND TOM Allen with Cynthia Dobson on the same beach where I had first met them. The ashes of the big bonfire were still there, cold and black in the noon sunlight. A winter light, the sea gray-green and ponderous on the rocky beach. The logs and driftwood lay in a circle like the dead people in this whole case, the charred remains of the circle of fire.

"You came back, Shaw?" Tom Allen said. He carried a handful of stones, threw them one by one out into the heavy sea.

"Is something wrong?" Cynthia Dobson asked. In the thin sunlight she was slim and very pretty with the wind blowing at her hair.

"Ben Wheeler hasn't been caught," I said. "He's hiding here in Fort Smith. It may not be over at all."

They looked at each other. Cynthia Dobson reached out to touch Tom Allen. Maybe they just wanted it to be all over, to forget the last weeks, get on with their lives.

"I want you to tell me about that last phone call of Dobson's that evening," I said. "He called about ten to six, said he'd see you in the morning? Did he say who he was with?''

"No," Tom Allen said.

"You didn't happen to call him at Sam MacGruder's and change your meeting place to The Pines?"

"No, we didn't," Cynthia Dobson said.

"Did he say why he was at The Pines?"

"No." Allen this time. "He just said that he had something better to do, had made a real juicy pickup."

" 'All of a sudden,' " I said. "That was how you told it to me the first time. Dobson said 'all of a sudden' he had something better to do."

"Yes, that's right." Tom Allen agreed.

" 'A chance too good to miss,' " I said.

Allen nodded. "That was it, yes."

"He had an appointment with you two at six-thirty, an important appointment. But he called it off at the last minute, almost, for a chance too good to miss. A pickup. Of a woman who had every reason *not* to accept a pickup. It isn't consistent that Lillian Marsak would have let herself be picked up under normal circumstances, and is it logical for Dobson to have *made* a pickup when he had his appointment with you?"

Tom Allen seemed puzzled. Cynthia Dobson laughed a nasty laugh, cynical.

"Russ would do anything for a woman. All a woman had to do was smile at him and he'd drool after her," Cynthia said.

"A chaser, yes. He could be counted on to go after any woman," I said, "but with an important appointment, involving money, would he really have made the advances?"

Cynthia Dobson hesitated. "Well—"

"Or could it have been Lillian Marsak who picked *him* up?"

They looked at each other again.

" 'A chance too good to miss'," I said. "Does that sound like a man who has just made a pickup, or a man who has been picked up? An offer made to *him?*"

"He was happy," Tom Allen said. "Almost laughing with glee. It could have been her who'd picked him up, yes."

Cynthia Dobson said, "That's something Russ just wouldn't ever turn down for any appointment."

"And people here knew that."

"Yes," Cynthia said, "almost anyone would have known that."

Tom Allen said, "You think someone planned to make Dobson be in that car with her when the bomb went off? No accident, after all? Murder, too?"

"Yes," I said. "I think Jack Ready knew that, too. Now Ben Wheeler knows."

45

THE MARKHAM ARMS was a shabbier place in the winter sunlight. The one young mother pushing her baby carriage wore a ragged old sweater. Virginia Piper opened the door when I rang at her cottage. She walked into her living room with me.

"What is it now? Haven't you got enough to do chasing poor Ben Wheeler?" the dark-haired girl said. Her pretty face was older—temporarily. She would bounce back, we all do, but at this moment she was feeling death in the air.

"Maybe Ben Wheeler's doing the chasing," I said.

"Chasing? Ben?"

She sat down, her elegant figure not at all older. The body doesn't change with moods, feelings of mortality. I sat down facing her.

"First we all assumed that Russell Dobson had been the main target," I said. "Then I proved he couldn't have been because it was a sudden pickup, but I made another assumption. I assumed Dobson had picked up Lillian. He didn't. She picked him up, Ginny. She did the pickup, and not because she wanted to take him home with her."

"She picked him up?"

"I'm sure of it," I said. "Think for me. Just how did it happen?"

She shook her head. "I was away phoning, and when I came back I joined another guy at a table. I never saw what went on before they got together."

"All right. But think about the time you and Lillian were alone before Dobson came into the bar. Did she say anything odd? Do anything? Act strange? You said she looked at her watch because of her six o'clock date with Ben Wheeler. Was there anything else at all?"

"I didn't know she was meeting Ben Wheeler, she didn't say that."

"All right. What did she talk about?"

"Nothing much. Girl talk. She was in a happy mood. Sort of laughing, looking around the bar a lot. I—" She stopped, seemed to think hard. "I . . . I sort of noticed her looking at the door when anyone came in. Not many did, you know? I didn't think about it much."

"As if she were expecting someone?"

"I guess. I suppose I thought it was whoever she was meeting at six, but it couldn't have been, could it?"

"No. She was meeting Ben Wheeler at her car," I said. "You say she was happy? She was going to meet Ben Wheeler, who'd made her angry bothering her, and tell him off, but she was happy, laughing?"

"Yes. She even bought my drinks."

"Was that usual?"

"No sir. Lil was tight. In fact, just the day before she'd been broke. Yes, that was funny, now that I think of it, you know? I mean, she'd been almost broke the day before, then she bought drinks, and I think she had money in her place when they looked, the cops. In her purse, too, what was left of it."

"How much money?"

"I'm not sure. Maybe a thousand in her place. The sheriff would know."

"Yes," I said. "Do you know where a Mrs. Della Kurtz lives?"

"No. I don't know anyone named Kurtz."

As I drove away from the Markham Arms I was sure now. Someone had paid Lillian Marsak to pick up Russell Dobson that evening. That explained the pickup that wasn't logical for Lillian Marsak. Not a pickup, a job. For money Lillian Marsak would have done it, yes. That she could have explained to Campbell Grant—if she had to.

All I needed now was to know who and why. I thought I had a good idea where I'd find both.

46

RUSSELL DOBSON'S OFFICE was deserted, the packed boxes
still piled all over the floor. I drove on to Pimiento Lane
and the big old house where Nancy Cathcart lived alone.
There was no answer to my ring. I turned away, wonder-
ing where to look for her next, and heard the sound.

A faint sound like something soft but heavy falling.

Inside the house.

I listened, but it didn't come again. I tried the front
door. It was locked. I went around to the side, and saw the
garage doors closed. I looked into the garage through a
window. Her car was in there.

I circled the house. The back door was locked, too. She
wasn't a woman who left her doors unlocked. I found an
open window at the rear. A kitchen window. I climbed
into a spotless kitchen that wasn't used much. The kitchen
of a woman who lived alone with a Puritan temperament.

I went through into the living room where we had
talked. It was empty, dust hanging in the musty air in the
brittle light of the winter sun through the curtained windows. I went on through the downstairs rooms. A small

rear room with a television set and comfortable old furniture was where Nancy Cathcart obviously spent most of her time at home.

I found her there.

She lay on her back on the carpeted floor in front of a big couch. There was blood on the couch, and on the front of it where she had rolled off onto the floor. There was some blood on the floor around her, but not too much. I bent over her, touched her. Her eyes had been closed. They opened.

"P . . . Paul . . . ?"

"Yes," I said. "How does it feel?"

She had been shot twice in the chest and head. Small wounds. She was alive, but for how long? Her breathing was heavy and shallow. It hurt. She closed her eyes again after the single look at me. Her face was drawn and very neutral. Nothing on her face at all as if she were holding very tight to herself to keep from moving a hair and losing her hold on any part of the life in her. If she moved it might slip away, slip out of her, the life. She moved her lips the barest fraction.

"It . . . hurts . . . Paul."

"Who was it?"

Only her eyelids fluttered for a negative shake. "I don't . . . know. In the doorway . . . coat . . . no face . . . shot . . ."

"No more," I said. "Don't move."

I found the telephone, called an ambulance and a doctor. Then I called Sheriff Quigley. His office said he was out. I told them. They would be here at once. I went back to Nancy Cathcart. She hadn't moved at all, her breathing still slow and very shallow. Her eyes were closed, her face in that almost inhuman neutrality. Thinking now of nothing but her pain and her life, the instant of each slow breath.

"Nancy," I said. "The ambulance is on its way. You'll be all right. Just listen to me. If I say something you want to say no to, open your eyes. That's all. If the answer to any question I ask is yes, don't do anything."

Her lips moved. ". . . why . . . shoot me?"

"Nancy." I kneeled down and bent close over her. "I know now that Russell Dobson's death was no accident, after all. You hear? No accident. Murder. A dirty, clever murder. Somehow the murderer knew that Ben Wheeler had put the bomb in Lillian Marsak's car. He *knew*, but instead of stopping Wheeler and saving Lillian Marsak, he used Wheeler's murder to murder Dobson for himself."

Her face showed no reaction. Her eyes unmoving, closed and hidden.

"Nancy? You hear me? Someone knew Ben Wheeler had put a bomb in Lillian Marsak's car, could have saved her, but let her die so that Russell Dobson would be killed. Jack Ready knew, so he's dead. You know something, so you're shot."

She breathed slowly and opened her eyes. Once. Closed them again.

"Nancy? Who wanted Dobson dead so much? Do you know?"

Her eyes opened, stared up, closed again.

"Nancy," I said. "That address in Pacific Palisades: 148 Ashford Way. It's the loose end, the piece that doesn't fit. My partner knew nothing, but he was shot. All he did was go to 148 Ashford Way. The letter Dobson got from there. It wasn't from any old buddy, was it?"

Her eyes opened again. I saw in them a different pain. An older, maybe more deadly, pain coming through the pain of her wounds. She was thinking now of more than holding onto her life.

"Campbell Grant didn't know what that address, that letter, meant, but you do. It disturbed you that Grant had told me about it. You know, don't you?"

She did nothing. The answer was yes.

"Who lived at 148 Ashford Way? What was that letter? Nancy, try to tell me now."

Her eyes opened. She moved—an inch. ". . . sister . . . she went—"

"The letter was from your sister?"

"Peggy . . . Dobson . . . love . . . ran to . . ."

"Your sister, Peggy, and Dobson ran off together to Los Angeles? That time a year ago when he was away in Los Angeles for a month, he was with your sister?"

Nancy Cathcart closed her eyes. Yes, her sister and Russell Dobson had lived together in Los Angeles a year ago. Her lips moved. So faintly. I had to lean down.

"Peggy . . . to be . . . married . . . met Dobson . . . love . . . ran off . . . then—"

"Your sister was going to get married, met Dobson, and ran off with him? Who was she going to marry, Nancy?"

". . . never knew . . . that some reason . . . a secret . . . she never . . . told me—"

"Who did she know here? What men?"

". . . love . . . Dobson . . . then . . . letter . . ."

Her face went suddenly quiet, the rigid neutrality gone. That desperate motionlessness to hold on to her slipping life relaxed, and her face became almost smiling, peaceful. I bent closer. She was still breathing. She had passed out from the pain, the effort.

I heard the ambulance siren suddenly very close. They would be here in a moment. The sheriff wouldn't be far behind. There would be questions, official channels to Los

Angeles. Time. I didn't want to lose any time. Already it could be too late, the clever killer who had used another man's murder to commit his own might be covering more tracks.

I went out the back, circled around to my car, drove for the airport.

There I had some luck. A 727 was going out right then, they had space. I checked all the passengers before I took my seat. There was no one I knew aboard.

All the way down, Nancy Cathcart's words were going through my mind: *"Peggy . . . to be . . . married . . . met Dobson . . . love . . . ran off . . . then—"* And the last few words again: *". . . love . . . Dobson . . . then . . . letter . . ."*

It was the one word, *"then,"* that was going around in my mind. That and something I remembered Nancy Cathcart saying earlier: *"I had a sister, Peggy. Two years older. There was a man who wanted to marry her, she said. She went off with someone else instead. He used her. She died."*

47

IT WAS HOTTER in Pacific Palisades. The late afternoon sun was bright on the garden-apartment complex on the rim of the canyon at 148 Ashford Way.

I saw no one around in the shadows, there were no cars parked on the street. The same little manager was behind the desk in his office. He was still friendly, smiled at me.

"So? Still after that fellow Dobson? I haven't thought of anything."

"Now I want to know about someone else. A woman. Peggy Cathcart."

He shook his head. "Sorry, no bell. I don't seem to be much help to you at all."

"She was a woman from Fort Smith, about thirty. Came here about a year ago, probably, was still here some nine months ago. That man, Russell Dobson, might have been saying he was her husband."

"It just doesn't mean anything, Mr. Shaw."

"Did anything happen here about nine months ago? A murder? A death? This woman—"

The little man sat up and suddenly swore. "Damn it, sure! Cathcart you said? Wait a minute."

He began to rummage in his desk drawers.

"Then there was a woman named Cathcart?"

"No, not her," he said, went on searching in his desk. "It was the sister. She was named Cathcart, I think. Hold on, yeh, here it is." He held up a slip of paper, a receipt. "Nancy Cathcart, that was the sister. She had to sign for the damn woman's things when she took them, not that there was much to take. The woman said her name was Smith, sure. What else except Smith? Only, she wasn't here any three or four months, no sir. A few days, but I won't forget her. Even her advance rent check bounced a week later. I had to write to the sister for the money."

"What happened?"

"Suicide. Killed herself with an overdose of pills. Dead two days when we found her, and she'd only been here three days. Must have come here just to kill herself. The suitcase she carried with her turned out to be empty. No identification on her at all."

"Then how did you find out who she was?"

"The sister. If she hadn't shown up we might not have even found her body until she began to stink."

"You mean you hadn't found her dead before the sister came here?"

"Right." The manager nodded. "The sister showed up three days after 'Mrs. Smith' rented the place. Seems the sister had a letter from this address saying that 'Mrs. Smith' would be dead when the sister got the letter. The sister came right down, we busted the door, and there she was—two days dead."

So that was the letter. A suicide note sent by a woman alone in a new apartment who knew that she would be dead before it was read. A letter not to Nancy Cathcart, but to Russell Dobson.

"Was the sister, Nancy Cathcart, alone when she came?"

"As far as I know. Wait. She did come in a car, maybe there was someone else behind the wheel."

"What happened after the dead woman was found?"

"Called the cops. Open-and-shut case. Door was even on the chain inside, windows all locked. No doubt it was a suicide. After a day, the sister took the body home. That was all."

"But you never saw a man with the sister?"

"Nope. No one ever came about her after that until you right now."

I could see it in my mind. Peggy Cathcart, jilted and deserted by Russell Dobson, living alone for almost three months somewhere in Los Angeles. Then, despairing, coming to this apartment to kill herself. Sending the letter that must have shaken Russell Dobson, if not for too long. But the result of it all had shaken someone else a lot more, and a lot longer.

"You have no idea where she was living before she came here? This Mrs. Smith?"

"Nope."

"Didn't the police ask about that?"

"Yeh, but I told them I didn't know, and the sister didn't either. They weren't much interested, it was a plain suicide."

A dead end? Where had Peggy Cathcart had her month with Russell Dobson? Where had she been in the three months or so between Dobson and her death? Why come here to . . .

"You said her check bounced?"

"Sure did. Deposit and two months' rent. I only charged the sister for the one month. I mean, I had to."

"You gave the check to the sister? Or to the police?"

"The check? Oh, you mean the bounced check? No, never thought about it. I mean, it was a week after, it was all closed."

"You wouldn't still have it? The bounced check?"

"Well, yeh, maybe I do. I keep those things, you never know."

He rummaged through his desk again as he talked. I waited. It was an off chance at best, but it was all I had unless Nancy Cathcart could tell me more when she recovered. That might be much too late.

"Here you are," the manager said.

I took the check. The name and address were printed on it: Mrs. Robert Smith, 62 Carter Place, Santa Monica.

48

IT WAS ANOTHER garden-apartment complex. The manager was a middle-aged woman this time. She smoked a cigarette in one corner of her mouth, the smoke rising and closing one eye.

"You bet I remember Mrs. Smith. Him, too. Nice woman, I thought. Didn't care much for him, though. Too smooth, too sure of himself."

"They were here three months?"

"She was. He was here about a month. Then she was alone. I always thought there was something funny about them, not that it was my business then. Two months she sat in that apartment all alone, hardly ever going out except to go to work. The last two weeks she didn't even go to work. She didn't pay the rent. I told her she had to pay in a week, or leave. I kept her stuff until she paid."

"No one else ever came? No man?"

"No one I ever saw," the woman-manager said. "Alone every night. Quit her job, or got fired, and then she sat up there alone all day. I gave her a week to pay, then she'd have to leave, I'd keep her stuff until she paid up. She walked out and never came back. I waited a week, cleaned

out her place and rented it. Left all her stuff, me in the bag
for three weeks' rent, and just never came back.''

"What happened to her things?"

"I still got them in storage. You want to see them?"

I wanted to see them.

"Pay me three weeks' rent, they're yours," the woman-
manager said.

49

W<small>HEN</small> S<small>HERIFF</small> Q<small>UIGLEY</small> and his men picked me up at the Fort Smith airport it wasn't quite ten o'clock. For the first few miles the sheriff's headlights swept the empty highway ahead.

"It was all there among her things," I said. "Letters, a diary. She lived with Russell Dobson in Santa Monica for one month. She was alone there for two months—no visitors, no letters. Then she just quit her job, sat alone, the rent fell behind, the manager gave her a week. She walked out, ended in that apartment in Pacific Palisades. Wrote a rubber check, sent her suicide letter to Russell Dobson and took her pills. Dobson and Nancy Cathcart went down, got the body, end of affair."

Sheriff Quigley drove steadily with his eyes fixed ahead on the deserted highway. "I never heard one word. Nancy Cathcart never told. Just that Peggy had died, Nancy brought her home to bury. Nothing about Russ Dobson."

"What good would it have done? Nancy is a proud woman, old family. It was over, why tell and expose her sister?"

"If she had told, she wouldn't be in the hospital now," Quigley said. "A lot of people might be alive. Damn people!"

We rode in silence for a few miles. The lights of the second car of deputies behind us played across our faces, lighted the interior of the sheriff's car as we drove closer to town with the shadows of the tall redwoods off to the side.

"It might have saved Nancy from getting hurt," I said. "No one else. When Peggy Cathcart killed herself down there, Russell Dobson was going to be murdered one way or another."

I saw the big neon sign of The Pines shining ahead a mile before we reached the roadhouse. Cars were going in and out of the parking lot, and the traffic on the road had suddenly grown to a steady stream.

"Vasto was going to marry Peggy Cathcart," I said. "It was in her letters, in her diary. They'd kept it quiet up here because of Vasto's wife. She's a full, good Catholic, if a bad wife. But for Peggy Cathcart, Vasto was going to get a divorce. Break with his religion, change his whole life, in his own mind even risk damnation. It was that important. Then Peggy Cathcart met Russ Dobson, ran off with him, and killed herself. Vasto must have hated Dobson as much as a man can hate."

We slowed, and turned into the crowded parking lot of Salvatore Vasto's roadhouse. We stopped, and the deputies came up to our car. Quigley told them to watch all the doors. Two of them would wait for Quigley at the front door. The sheriff lit a cigarette, made no move to get out of the car.

"Jack Ready must have seen Ben Wheeler making that bomb," Quigley said, smoked and watched the brightly lighted roadhouse. "Probably afraid to tackle Big Ben alone. Went to Vasto, the boss, for help. Vasto said he'd handle Wheeler, I guess."

"Instead," I said, "Vasto watched Wheeler, learned about Big Ben meeting Lillian Marsak at six o'clock that evening. Vasto knew about the bomb, it was easy to know what Ben Wheeler was going to do at six o'clock that night. He had one of his waitresses call Dobson at Sam MacGruder's place, then asked Dobson to come to The Pines bar. Vasto'd already paid Lillian Marsak to pick up Dobson, take Dobson home in her car. Lillian didn't know the car was wired for a bomb, and Russ Dobson would never refuse such an invitation. A good gamble, and if Dobson hadn't gone with Lillian, Vasto'd just have tried again later.

"But it worked, Dobson was dead. Only Jack Ready knew anything, and he wouldn't talk because of Ben Wheeler. Smart, and cold-blooded—using another man's murder to commit your own. Vasto really hated Dobson. Cold, blind, ferocious hate."

Quigley swore softly in the car. "He was double-safe. We all assumed it was Dobson who'd been bombed, and for politics. As long as we thought politics, nothing could lead us to Sal Vasto. If we got smart, we'd find out about Ben Wheeler and Lillian, and blame it all on Wheeler alone. Vasto all safe."

"You had doubts about the politics," I said. "He didn't fool you that far."

"Far enough," Quigley said.

"No, not far enough for Vasto, and that's when he made his mistake. I suppose Campbell Grant made too much fuss, maybe even threatened out loud to get outside help. Whatever, when Grant came to us in Los Angeles, Vasto had him followed. You said once that Jack Ready had the connections to hired gunmen, and so does Vasto. His hired men tailed my partner to the Pacific Palisades address. That scared Vasto—his motive might be found. So he had my partner shot, sent men for me at Bodega Bay."

"But you made it here," Quigley said, "and Vasto knew the political motive for Dobson's murder wouldn't hold up to a real study."

"So he decided to 'help' me discover Ben Wheeler and

Lillian Marsak, even let Big Ben stumble around after me, and finally told me all about Ben Wheeler. Who would look farther once we had Ben Wheeler?"

"Except it left him with Jack Ready who wasn't about to stay quiet if Ben Wheeler was caught," Quigley said. "Vasto had to kill Jack Ready then. Probably planned to kill you out at the cabin if you'd learned the truth. But you hadn't, you were chasing Big Ben, so he killed Jack Ready and left. Sure we'd all be sure that Wheeler had killed Jack Ready, too."

"Only—Wheeler got away and knew that *he* hadn't killed Jack Ready. So Wheeler didn't run, stayed here. Maybe he knows who killed Jack Ready, his only friend, or maybe he's trying to find out. What mattered is that I realized Wheeler hadn't killed Jack Ready. When I went to Vasto today, he saw that I was very close to the real truth. That left Vasto with his motive—he had to cover the motive now. Only Nancy Cathcart could lead me to the motive, so Vasto shot her. This time he failed, she didn't die."

"Yes," Quigley said. "We better get him."

The two deputies followed us into the crowded, bright roadhouse. The bar was packed, noisy. Quigley stopped at the bar. The bartender who had been on duty that evening Dobson and Lillian Marsak died came up to the sheriff.

"Where's Vasto?" Quigley said.

"His office, I guess. Ain't seen him," the bartender said.

Quigley nodded his two deputies back toward the entrance to Salvatore Vasto's office corridor. The bartender, Marco, watched, looked at me. His face was expressionless.

"Shaw asked you if Russell Dobson mentioned anyone else the night he was killed," Quigley said to the bartender. "Now I'm asking, Marco. Officially. Did Dobson ask for anyone?"

Marco looked at me, at the two deputies waiting in the rear near Vasto's office corridor. "He asked for Mr. Vasto.

He said the boss had called him to come here. Mr. Vasto told me not to tell anyone.''

We went back to where the two deputies waited. The new young man was at the guard table.

"You want something, Sheriff?"

"Vasto," Quigley said. "He in his office?"

"Guess so. He ain't been out yet tonight. I'll tell—"

"No, you won't," Quigley said.

A deputy stood with the young muscle man. We walked down the corridor to Salvatore Vasto's office. It was unlocked. Inside it was empty. Quigley swore.

"Damn! He's gone. Must have—"

"Sheriff," I said.

The inner door in the side wall that led to Vasto's private wine cellar was open. Quigley took out his gun, nodded to his deputy. I had my gun. Quigley went down the dark stairs first. There was light at the bottom.

It was a small cellar lined with wine racks, the rows of dusty bottles all lying on their sides. We saw nothing but the racks of wine. We went down the rows until we reached a hidden corner behind the last row.

Salvatore Vasto sat in a wooden chair, his staring eyes turned up showing only the whites, his tongue lolling out of his mouth with a trickle of blood. His head rested on his left shoulder at a grotesque angle, dark bruises on his neck.

Ben Wheeler sat on the dirt floor against a wall next to the dead roadhouse owner. The massive man had his eyes closed, his left leg stuck straight out, caked black blood all over his ripped trousers. I could smell the gangrene even from ten feet away. A heavy, putrid odor that filled the small cellar.

A small pistol lay on the floor near Salvatore Vasto's dead feet. A hole in the masonry wall low down showed where Ben Wheeler had tunneled through from the main cellar. Some cans of food lay open and empty near the big man, and a worn deck of playing cards. The big man had tunneled through, and waited for Salvatore Vasto. He had played cards with himself, eaten, sat with his leg festering for a whole day or more, sure that sooner or later Salvatore Vasto would come down for wine.

"Ben?" Quigley said.

There was nothing to say to Salvatore Vasto. The road-house owner had had his neck broken, snapped in the grip of the big man's massive hands.

"Ben?" Quigley said. "It's the sheriff."

The big man opened his eyes. Dying eyes, the gangrene too far gone. Or maybe it was just his will that was too far gone. A kind of broken pain in his dull eyes, suffering confusion.

"He killed Jack," Ben Wheeler said, a hoarse whisper. "He was out there. I saw him. Why'd he kill Jack?"

"It's all right, Ben," Quigley said. "He used you both, maybe he had it coming. We'll go now, get you fixed up."

"Why'd he have to go kill Jack?" Ben Wheeler said. His dull, pained eyes were crying. Tears that rolled down. "He didn't have to go kill Jack."

Quigley motioned to his deputy to stay with Ben Wheeler, picked up the small pistol that lay on the floor.

"Looks like the gun Vasto used on Nancy Cathcart," the sheriff said. "We'll check it out. I'll call in, Shaw, you go send my deputies all down to get Ben Wheeler. We'll need an ambulance."

"He won't make it, Sheriff," I said.

"I guess he won't really mind," Quigley said.

He used the phone in Salvatore Vasto's office, while I rounded up his deputies, sent them down to Ben Wheeler. I waited at the car. The ambulance was already wailing off in the distance when Quigley came out to the car.

"I forgot to ask," he said, "how's your partner?"

"Out of danger now. I called when I was down in Los

Angeles," I said. "One victim Sal Vasto didn't get, at least."

"Yeh," Quigley said. "But he got one more. Nancy Cathcart died in the hospital an hour ago."

Is there a logic in the world? I don't know. Locked tight inside herself, Nancy Cathcart had refused me one night when she had wanted me, wanted a man. Two nights I had failed to go to her. Would she have died any happier if I had gone, if she had let me be with her? Could I have helped her? A passing ship. Or had she died as she had lived, to herself? At least escaped her sister's anguish?

Quigley was looking up and across the highway toward the tall shadows of the giant redwoods. "You know, I might just decide to run for that senate seat against Jesse Boetter, Tom Allen and Campbell Grant. Next time. Men have to live, yes, but so do those trees."

"If I lived here, I'd vote for you," I said.

I would. I thought about it all the way back to Quigley's office where they had brought my car from the airport. He was the one man I had met in Fort Smith who might be able to help in a world that had formed a Salvatore Vasto who could have saved Lillian Marsak's life, but had used her life instead to feed his hate of Russell Dobson. Used the anguish of one human being, and the death of another, to kill a third.

That Salvatore Vasto himself had been consumed in the circle of fire he had ignited didn't help much, he hadn't been worth one of his victims, and I tried to put it out of my mind as I drove south next morning to Los Angeles, and, soon, Maureen.

About the Author

Mark Sadler is an Edgar-winner, recipient of The Lifetime Achievement Award of The Private Eye Writers Of America, Shamus nominee and Past President of PWA. His books about modern private detective Paul Shaw reveal the rough side of our smooth world, the darkness and violence under the normal day-to-day surface. Under his other name of Michael Collins, he writes the famous adventures of PI Dan Fortune, and has received many international honors. A former New Yorker, Sadler and his wife, novelist Gayle Stone, live in Santa Barbara, California.